XISLE

a novel

by

Tamsin Spencer Smith

ISBN: 978-1-7329439-5-7

This novel is a work of fiction. Certain institutions, agencies, and public offices are mentioned, but the characters involved are wholly imaginary. With the exception of certain known historical facts and famous personages mentioned, any resemblance to actual events or figures is entirely coincidental. The Platt Amendment, the Cuban Revolution, and the ongoing political engagement of Miami Dade County's exile community, however, are certainly real.

Grateful acknowledgement is made to RiskPress Foundation for making The Divers Collection possible.

Cover Artwork by Jerry Lyles

Author Photo by David Smith

San Francisco, California

My Island, fragrant Island, flower of islands: hold me forever, give birth to me forever, pluck off all my departures one by one.

And keep the last for me, hidden under a little sun-warmed sand. On the shores of the Gulf where the hurricanes always make their mysterious nest!

Dulce Maria Loynaz, "Poema CXXIV"

Time is rhythm: the insect rhythm of a warm humid night, brain ripple, breathing, the drum in my temple – these are our faithful timekeepers; and reason corrects the feverish beat.

Vladimir Nabokov, *Ada*

To hope til Hope creates from its own wreak the thing it contemplates...

Percy Bysshe Shelley, *Prometheus Unbound*

AUTHOR'S NOTE

This book was written in Washington, D.C. in 1996, as I was finishing a six-year stint working as a legislative assistant for the U.S. House of Representatives. It doesn't seem that long ago, but in those days, few regular citizens used the Internet and Super PACs were not yet ubiquitous. My one claim to fame during this relatively brief career as a congressional aide involved the temporary suspension of funding for Radio and TV Marti, the American government's propaganda broadcasts directed against Fidel Castro. I also got into a spot of trouble over a provision requiring federal agencies to begin disclosing the ongoing cost of classifying records confidential, secret, and top secret.

This story unfolded as I walked to and from work on Capitol Hill. I'd jot down notes, then type them up at the end of each day. The tale has always felt to me more like a film than a novel. But, for now, these pages are the place where its characters lived and loved, lost and found. It didn't seem right to leave them alone with their secrets any longer. Here is a story that my younger self wanted to tell.

Tamsin Spencer Smith
San Francisco, 2020

XISLE

A PROLOGUE: THE LESSER OF TWO EVILS

Picture a petty thief. Imagine you watch as he deftly navigates the slim ledge above Roaster's Coffee House. He pauses, partially obscuring the shop's rough-hewn sign: "Waking up Capitol Hill since 1974." *A popular year for such efforts; but I digress. The subject in question – our wall hugging hoodlum – is oblivious to the footprints of history. His attention is fastened to the here and now. Specifically, to the contents of the room he's peering into.*

He looks through the grimy windowpane, searching for snatchable items like mobile phones, laptop computers, and handbags. Easily pawnable prospects are his preferred prey. An experienced loot-lifter, it doesn't take him long to size-up the layout. Devoid of a law firm's smug grandeur or the self-conscious trappings of a personal office, he identifies the space in his sights as a common area. The scruffy appearance of the room further indicates this to be a kind of intern pool, in which the ambitions of many an eager apprentice crash against post-collegial proving grounds. Our bandit's hopes are plummeting.

The clincher, convincing him to look elsewhere for ready booty, is a collection of placards in the room's far corner. Emblazoned in green and blue lettering, they identify the organization to which these interns are attached: CITIZENS FOR OPEN GOVERNMENT. With no prior knowledge of COG's particular mission, our boy makes a calculated guess. He's crooked in the District of Columbia long enough to be well-schooled in one unbending maxim. Non-profit land is definitely <u>not</u> where the

1

money is. Public interest outfits trade in a different kind of currency.

Poor disappointed pilferer, he's chosen the wrong tree to shake. The ripe fruit lie to the north and west. He should have known to stick to K Street, where tasseled loafers outnumber Birkenstocks ten-to-one and even the grunts carry multiple gadgets. Grumbling to himself, the frustrated felon slips stealthily from his voyeur's perch. He eases down into Roasters for a double espresso and settles into reverie. Lost in a fantasy about large endowments more physical than fiscal, he's lost all interest in what's occurring back in the second-story space he's just been spying. The fickle voyeur is too easily distracted. It's a pity though, as a rather interesting story is about to unfold upstairs.

Readers wishing to follow the exploits of the hoodlum may elect to do so by periodically checking the local paper, where metropolitan crime stories are chronicled daily. Yet, for those preferring a longer lesson on larceny, in all its twisted forms, cast your ballot for a return to COG's chambers. Imagine again that humble workplace of political reform. Return your attention to the room above Roasters. It is here that our story begins.

Chapter 1

BUCKDANCER'S CHOICE

Lunch hour in the intern pit had struck, and the hive was on the move. A singular figure fought against the current. The hoard, either sensing authority or opting for the path of least resistance, adopted a V-formation to allow his passage. Within moments of entering, the man found himself abandoned. He turned to leave, but a noise from the squeak of a chair announced that he was not alone. One intern remained. *Squeak.* She was using the phone cord to swivel herself back and forth. Long neck. Fair skin. Long, fair hair and an admirable profile. He waited for her to finish.

The man himself stood over 6-feet tall with broad shoulders and bright eyes. A pencil behind one ear kept dark waves from covering his face. He angled his body gracefully against a desk, though his hands remained in perpetual motion. Catching this tick, he slid them into his pockets, as he waited to speak with the young woman, who was still unaware of his presence.

His ears tuned to the sound of her voice. She was giving a quick-and-dirty critique of the Washington job market. The words pulled him back to his own stint as a lowly intern at COG. Several years and numerous promotions separated him from those indignities, but the female voice a few feet away, rung true.

"...it *is* a real job" Ada Tremont sighed into the phone. "Just because I'm not..." She winced at some comment from the other end of the line, then continued wearily: "Whatever, Dad. It's not a waste of time. I'd rather be paying my dues at this office than some other."

Another sigh. "Okay, I'll do that. Yep. Fine. Let's just agree that you'll hang in there and I'll do the same."

Squeak.

"Love you too."

She put the phone down, smiled to herself and took a long stretch. She'd been sitting cat-like, with her legs tucked in a pre-pounce position atop her desk chair. Making yet another squeaky swivel, she pulled herself up. Long legs unbending to stand, she propped her elbows on the cubby divider, expecting to catch a wink or at least a head shake from a sympathetic peer. Instead, her eyes alit upon an unfamiliar face. He looked relaxed, but decidedly not intern-like. Must be one of those with – as her dad would have put it – a "real job" at Citizens for Open Government.

"Did you need something, sir?" she asked, stepping towards him. "I apologize. I was just talking with my father, explaining why he's still subsidizing me through my post-academic years. Do you need an errand run?"

"No. Er. Actually, yes. I came down here looking for a hand, but then I overheard you on the phone," he smiled, "I used to have your job. Way back when."

"Can't have been *that* long ago."

Laughing: "You're most kind. I started as an intern in this very room actually. I never minded gophering, but I had a friend with the poor taste to nickname me 'Lancelot.' You know, quest for the Holy Grail and all that."

She grinned, "I feel much better." Extending her hand, "Lance, then?"

"Sure," leaning in conspiratorially, "but why don't you try Peter round the office."

"I'm Ada."

"Ada, how long have you been here in the intern pit?"

"Just shy of two weeks."

He nodded slowly for some seconds. He hooked a thumb in the direction of the door. Therewith, Peter Vane, Director of Policy at COG made Ada Tremont an offer she couldn't refuse.

"How'd you like to give up interning for a while and come help out as my research assistant? It even comes with a salary."

"You really are my knight in shining armor." She beamed, "lead the way."

5

As they strode out together, Ada mused to herself, looks like I owe you one, Dad.

Peter was thinking much the same thing, but not for this or any of the more obvious reasons.

UNANIMOUS CONSENT

June bugs, he called them. The bartender had been observing this seasonal migratory phenomenon for long enough to take note. It was his third summer manning the rail at *Unanimous Consent*, a lively bar in Adams-Morgan, the trendiest of Washington neighborhoods. Here the fresh faces of America's future passed their evenings in libation and flirtation.

The bartender had developed an accurate, though unscientific, system for classifying his customers according to type.

New England liberals gravitated towards the think tanks; wide-eyed Midwesterners tended to seek positions on the staffs of their hometown Congressional representatives; Southerners seemed to end up in lobbying firms, hired to protect farm subsidies and defense contracts; cynical New Yorkers fell naturally into muckraking. But West Coasters were loose cannons. Never could tell if a kid from California would be more interested in protecting an endangered species or persecuting the undocumented.

For the most part, he considered, if you monitor bar traffic, you can become a pretty solid judge of where your patrons come from and where they're headed. But tonight, the amateur barkeep-cum-political demographer was having a tough time sizing up the pretty female sitting front and center at the beer taps. She'd been there roughly 20 minutes and hadn't once looked at her watch or spun around in the stool to check the neon clock on the far wall. Damned unusual. People tended to act antsy and self-conscious when kept waiting alone in a bar. Yet this woman looked serene as can be. He wondered why she was there. She must be waiting for someone. Legs like that don't go unchased.

QUORUM

Finally, the crew arrived. Ada and her grad school companions spent the first few minutes of their reunion at the bar reminiscing about their years together in the bubble of Stanford University. A mandatory round of shameless self-promotion and one-upmanship quickly followed. Just like old times.

As expected, Kara – known to the group as Kermit – was thrilled about her new dream job at Ocean World.

"Sounds like a theme park," quipped the friend seated to her right.

"It's a nationally-recognized environmental organization, Quinn, as you very well know." She continued undaunted, enthusiastically detailing her hopes of traveling to far-flung lands and participating in various global conferences. She described her coworkers as earnest and friendly. Even better, some looked to be promising prospects for interoffice romance. The only complaint she saw fit to voice concerned her dismally low salary.

"Pay on the Hill is pretty dismal too," added Jaime, leaning back to compose a toothy smile, "mind you, I ain't complaining."

'Nor should you! And congratulations, by the way," Kermit squeezed his arm.

"A toast to Jaime for scoring his dream job."

"Here, here," in unison.

Through diligence, luck and no small amount of chutzpah, Jaime had secured a post as Legislative Assistant to Congressman Richard Peralta, an active member of the Foreign Affairs

Committee. To get there, he'd toiled two summers as an unpaid fellow in the Congressman's personal office, impressing the powers that be with his dedication and understanding of international issues. When Peralta's Committee staffer announced her acceptance of a post with the State Department, Jaime's hard work was rewarded. Street smarts had taught him how to get himself into the right place at the right time. He'd fought off interoffice rivals by making himself indispensable, playing the Washington power game the way a kid with no family connections or other easy "ins" had to.

The only sour note to the reunion's general revelry was their buddy Dan's random attacks on seemingly every line of conversation. His swipes were particularly vicious regarding politicians, especially those who "stuck their noses in" on foreign and military matters. Jaime's new boss wasn't attacked directly, but the hostility of his commentary made them all uncomfortable. And it caught them off-guard.

Unfortunately, Dan's once refreshingly non-PC attitude had undergone a radical reformulation after he accepted a position as a research associate with the Dulles Center. The Center was a controversial policy institute, whose reactionary positions on national security issues had precipitated a number of highly publicized scandals involving covert campaigns against leftist revolutionaries in Latin America and Africa during the 1980s. Time in the echo chamber seemed to be taking a toll.

Thus far, no one had engaged Dan, but Ada could see Jaime struggling to hold his tongue. She sought to steer the conversation to calmer waters by encouraging Lindy to give an update.

"Hey what's the deal with that new anchorman's hair-do? Looks like a leather shower cap."

"Yeah, it's a thing to behold." Lindy launched into a lively series of anecdotes about her work behind-the-scenes on the Channel Nine News Hour. Her stories of lecherous guest pundits, pathological hosts, and rampant backstabbing among the production staff had them all laughing again and signaling for another pitcher of beer.

Quinn was the only one who had remained relatively silent throughout. Ada wondered whether any of the others knew of his decision to blow off a stack of top-notch job offers to join the investigative team at the watchdog journal *Beltways*. Not only had Quinn been the sharpest mind in their year at Stanford, he was also impeccably well plugged in. His father, after serving nearly three decades in the U.S. Senate, had settled into a patrician's life of serving on distinguished boards and positioning his only son for greatness. Quinn had dutifully shown up at all the pre-arranged interviews, suitably dazzled perspective employers and, as expected, received various coveted invitations to employment. But Quinn didn't want to serve the powers that be, not even the one he called dad.

Ada and Quinn had been instant friends and eventually lovers. She admired him and loved his dry humor, quick mind and candid speech. Plus, his sandy hair, blue eyes, surfer's slouch, and the way he touched her. Ada could see only one defect in their relationship, but it was a defining one. She knew their respective private ambitions would always take precedence over a collective destiny. Either of them was capable of running off at the drop of a hat in pursuit of adventure; and the other, it was understood, would be left free to do the same.

Ada was still pondering love's ironies when she felt something cold and wet against her face. Quinn moved his beer bottle away from her cheek as the rest of them had a good laugh at her expense.

"Care to join, Ada?" he asked.

She gave his knee a squeeze, "I do."

"Well now that you're back," Jaime prodded, "why don't you fill us in on your latest. Have you decided what you want to be when you grow up?"

"Not sure I want to grow up, but I can feel my career path kicking up some sand."

"Are you finally being put to better use at COG?"

"Indeed. I've been moved up from grub level."

"Our little butterfly!"

Ada winked as she refilled her glass.

POINT OF ORDER

Dan, Kermit and Lindy begged off on Quinn's bid for another pitcher and said their goodbyes. Ada and Jaime hung around. While Quinn was at the bar, Jaime probed Ada for more detail.

"What's Peter Vane like in person? He's got a rep as a mover and shaker."

"Not what you'd expect. At least, he's not what I would have expected. Then again, I didn't know anything about him. Frankly, I'm surprised to hear that you do. What's the scoop?" It riled her a bit that Jaime seemed to know more than she about the man for whom she was already putting in overtime. But curiosity won out over pride. With a playful pout she chided, "And why, if he has such a big name, didn't you put me on his trail when I took the COG internship in the first place? I thought we kept no secrets between us."

Jaime laughed. "You'll do well in this town."

They were clinking beer mugs as Quinn slid back into the booth next to Ada.

Jaime explained: "I was just about to tell our butterfly here that I hadn't given her the low-down on Peter Vane when she joined his organization, in part because it's not my job to do her digging for her, but mostly because I never imagined they'd meet. I mean, who would have thought he'd be descending to the intern pit to pluck her up as a personal protégé."

Quinn could feel her eyes on him. He filled in the details he could sense she now needed and wanted. "Peter Vane may not be running COG yet, but he probably has more influence than the guy currently at the helm. Vane's single-handedly turned around the public interest research outfit, which had previously spent most of its time churning out dull research papers that no one but policy wonks ever read. Vane has a knack for packaging public scandal, as well as unearthing it."

Quinn paused. He knew she'd have wished to be the one enlightening the crowd about the boss for whom she was no doubt getting prouder by the minute. He was familiar with the glint he now saw in Ada's gray eyes; and continued: "Money's always played a role in politics and a corrupt connection between the two is nothing new. But the amount of dollars involved in today's campaigns has become staggering and the public's cynicism about Washington is off-the-charts. Put the two together and campaign finance reform is a blockbuster hit. Peter Vane as the taxpayer's action hero."

"PAC Slayer?!"

"Electorate Avenger?!"

"The Denominator?!"

"Ug! They're getting worse."

"It's late."

"Indeed."

"Is that a rap?"

"Stage left."

MORNING HOUR

Ada rose early with the sun. She stood at the open bedroom window looking out across the reddening treetops of Rock Creek Park. The oppressive humidity that turned the Potomac River into a swamp in Summer, had finally given way to the cooler air and warmer hues of Autumn.

As she brushed her teeth, Ada planned the Saturday ahead. Coffee. Run. Then into the office. What a difference a week can make, she thought, amazed that she didn't feel the slightest bit put out by the idea of working on such a glorious day. Learning last night what inside Washington thinks of Peter Vane had added kick to her drive. She was determined to impress him, her friends, and maybe even her father.

By 10:30 a.m., she was wired on French Roast, endorphins, and ambition. Freshly showered, knapsack loaded, and bike at the ready, she scrawled off a quick note and pinned it eye-level to the wall. As she opened the door to exit, a hand appeared to push it shut and encircle her waist. She wiggled and giggled, and tried to peel the fingers loose, protested in breathy gasps. Her captor silenced these cries by covering her lips with his own.

Shifting position, Quinn nodded towards her note: "So you say you're sneaking off to work today? Something's fishy here."

"No teasing, now," Ada said, pushing him away playfully. "Did you just get up to give me a hard time?"

"Guilty as charged."

"Well," she taunted, pulling at his T-shirt, "you know there's a penalty for that."

"Give a man his best destiny." With that he bent down and lifted her over his shoulder. "Come, my spirited siren, to meet our fate."

"You know I hate being carried."

"Light as a lotus blossom," Quinn observed as he set her down on the bed and began undressing her.

"Okay, but quick."

He smiled and looked up across her belly. He could see her eyes closed and mouth slightly open. He rested his cheek against her thigh and sighed, "You're beautiful when you're happy."

"I'm happy, I'm happy," she whispered.

MOTION TO INSTRUCT

It hadn't taken Ada long to realize that making one's mark can require blood, sweat, and tears. Ada had made it through the tears in the first weeks of her arrival in Washington. She could laugh about it now, her brief stint at the *Happy Hands Temp Agency*. She'd quit after ten days in utter desperation; there had been too many near escapes from seedy office managers.

She'd felt lucky to land the internship at COG. No one pressed against her at the copy machine and the work mattered. She liked the peers she'd met, and it seemed like intellect was valued and respected, even if it wasn't compensated. Then along came Peter Vane.

Hard work it was. Without a doubt, the project Peter had given her was far from glamorous. It involved the kind of painstaking research that defines tedium. She was to pour over Federal Election Commission filings, Congressional vote tallies, Committee hearing records, and innumerable trade press publications, in search of connections. The line separating political participation and undue influence can be hard to trace, but she was to look for instances in which the nexus between a campaign contribution and a politician's actions is too clear and too serious to ignore. It was Ada's job to connect the dots and plot where, why, and how dollars begat votes.

Peter Vane's orders had been light on specifics, heavy on metaphor. "I smell a rat," he said, handing Ada her assignment: "follow the droppings, then we'll run our own traps."

Ada took his oblique instructions as the sign of a loner. No stranger to such tendencies, she'd taken it as a challenge – leeway to prove herself. She'd read Peter's personality accurately. But in this case, his brevity had a certain cause. The "project" was a spur of the moment creation. Nostalgia had prompted him to invite her assistance. Thinking quickly, he'd devised an investigation – or rather, remembered a long-dormant desire to dig in a very particular ditch. He handed her the proverbial shovel and wondered what she'd find.

The sweat phase had begun, and Ada wanted to do well. The outlines were vague but hey, that's what instincts are for. She plunged in and settled herself on the floor amid piles of raw data.

Four hours in, Ada heard the sound of the elevator door, then steps, and the jangling of keys. In walked Peter Vane himself. They exchanged surprised-to-find-you-here hellos. In that split second of semi-awkward silence, she caught herself wondering how he'd spent the morning. The helmet in his hand told her he'd biked to work. Her own early a.m. activities flashed through her mind. Humm, best not speculate.

For his part, Peter had not expected to find her there sprawled amidst a mountain of paper. "Ada, you shouldn't be inside on such a beautiful day? Didn't I steal enough of your time during the work week?"

She blushed, scooting her bare feet beneath her.

"Um, I just wanted to work."

"Great." Peter stepped inside her paper moat. "Me too."

Ada patted the floor. "Perfect timing. I could use some guidance.

"How about a bonfire," he deadpanned.

"The oxygen to kindling ratio isn't optimal."

He laughed and moved to the window. "Let's get some circulation going. You must have been suffocating in all this dusty pulp."

The window flew up with clatter, spraying paint chips and sending the room's contents a-swirl. "Been a while," he grinned.

Ada laughed and Peter joined her on the floor. "Okay, I've gone through the latest FEC filings and identified top contributors to Senators and Congressmen of both parties. I'm matching these against legislation that's moving through committee or getting media play." She paused, glancing at her notes, then continued, "Most of what I've found is pretty standard stuff – financial lending institutions kicking in for Members on the Banking Committee, the Israeli-American Political Action Committee bestowing generosity on the folks that write foreign aid bills; Christian groups supporting pro-lifers…."

"Anything you wouldn't expect?" Peter asked.

"Yeah, one money trail seemed pretty long and wide, but I haven't been able to pin down its mission. Seems sort of random. The corporate PAC of Santos Fiesta Cruise Lines has been pouring lots of cash into the pockets of legislators, mostly from Florida and New Jersey, but also to people on the authorization and appropriations subcommittees that handle State Department programs. I had just started a database search on the company's founder when you came in. Apparently, this Miguel Santos built the business from scratch. It's been a very lucrative venture; he's way up there on Forbes wealthiest list. You'd figure he'd do better to spend his dough trying to influence the Transportation Committee or to get tax breaks out of Ways and Means. But he isn't. I can't see a smart business rationale for these contributions. Must be one though, I'd imagine this Santos didn't get rich making dumb investments."

You got that right, thought Peter. He leaned back and said: "Good work, Ada."

"Really?"

Peter stood up and started flipping through the Rolodex on his desk. He wrote something onto a slip of paper and handed it to her. "This is where you go next," he said.

Ada looked down and read: Franklin Aristotle Wayne 201 Dunbarton St. NW

"No phone number?" she asked.

Peter gave her a wry smile. "No, just knock. Tell him Lancelot sent you."

Chapter 2

SUMMER 1958

The eyes of the lovers filled with stars. Waves tickled the fringe at the foot of the sea-soaked blanket where they lay like castaways on a forgotten stretch of sand.

After many moments, the woman spoke. "Should they not return to town? Her parents would worry and hadn't he things to do?"

"Please, a few more minutes," the young man begged. Only 12 hours remained before he would return to America. He hoped to press the memory of the evening in his mind.

"Have faith," she said. "A few short months is not long to wait. Patience in exchange for a lifetime of happiness is not much to ask. They must trust. All will be well. A few short months and all will be well."

They rose and walked slowly along the shore. "Caro, mi amor," he whispered, "Caro, Caro, you cost me my heart."

"Querido, it was only mine to take, she replied, just as my heart will never beat for any other. Never." she promised.

He took her hand and held it to his chest.

WHAT'S IN A NAME

He talked, and as he talked
Wallpaper came alive;
Suddenly ghosts walked
And four doors were five.

Georgetown's 201 Dunbarton turned out to be a quaint red brick
row house in the federal style ubiquitous throughout that historic
section of the district. Yet, the home's exterior didn't tell Ada much
about its inhabitant. She wouldn't have been so curious, if Peter
had given any indication of what to expect. His instructions were,
as she was coming to recognize, typically nebulous. They left her
feeling slightly ridiculous standing at a stranger's front door with
little more than the name Peter Vane as a reference. Oh, what the
hell, she muttered pressing the button. A deep reverberating boom
intoned her presence.

A Gong? Brace yourself, she thought. Expect the unexpected of
Franklin Aristotle Wayne. The name itself demanded pause. How
does one get a grasp on a handle like that? On the cab ride over,
Ada had conceived an indistinct image in her mind, a portrait of an
eccentric scholar replete with spectacles, toga, and a six-shooter.
This phantom vision was banished as soon as the door opened.

A man of sixty or so, deeply tanned and very handsome cast his
pale eyes up-and-down Ada's tall frame.

"I don't yet know who you are, but it is a pleasure to find you
gracing my doorstep. Is your presence here accidental or

intended?" Bowing slightly, he added, "Stealing presumption, I'll add that my hopes rest on the latter."

"You certainly know how to put a stranger at ease, sir. I actually do have a reason for disturbing you, though I'm not precisely sure what it is."

Before she could continue, he stepped aside and led her in. They passed through a hallway, lined on all sides with masks, weapons, and various other artifacts. He guided her towards an impressively appointed study lined with modernist paintings and more indigenous art.

Her host began to point out certain items, bringing them to life with tales about their origins and his adventures in acquiring them. Each relic opened a window to a place beyond her experience, a lost realm growing richer in his stories of the bow & arrow sets of Brazilian Yanomami Indians and the Wayana of Suriname, the ceremonial penis gourds of Papua New Guinea, the painted paddles of French Guiana, the spears of Madagascar's Antandroy, and the blow guns of Venezuela's Makiritari.

As fascinating as the contents were, the man who'd collected them was more so. Though obviously American, he seemed exotic. His thick mane of snow-white hair made her think of a creature wild and feline.

He had been studying her with interest when she emerged from her reverie. Ada cast her eyes about the room, bringing them to rest on his. Turning to a low table by his side, he poured a greenish mixture into a glass and handed it to her.

"Thank you," she said accepting the drink. A moment passed between them. Ada broke the quiet. "So, I've learned that you're a traveler."

"In the old days, I roamed," he replied. "Now I just conjure up memories with the help of visual aids," he said, gesturing at the room's eclectic contents, "and redolent recipes." Raising his glass by way of illustration, he explained, "My afternoon *mojito,* limeade with a Caribbean twist."

Ada took a sip. A twist? More like a tornado, she thought. A full glass of this stuff and they'll be naming tropical storms after me. "Very nice, sir, thank you."

He chuckled. "You can't keep calling me sir, it's making me feel ancient and right now, I rather have a yen to be a few decades younger. So, it's Frank, okay?"

"Yes, of course. Frank. I haven't even introduced myself. I'm Ada Tremont." She started once more to explain the reason, still not entirely clear in her own mind, for her visit. But was again prevented from doing so.

"Ada Tremont. What a lovely name. Easy grace. I'm jealous. Mine is rather unruly, the result of a mother's over-subscribed expectations. She wanted me to be anything but the free-spirited adventurer that my father Bill Wayne was, so she tried to give me a pragmatist's destiny. She longed for a son to observe the moral prescriptions of *Poor Richard's Almanac* and to maintain the mental discipline of a philosophical rationalist. Unfortunately for her, it didn't work. For better or worse, genes don't take rewrites. The Wayne part won out."

Ada played along. "Well, I suppose that's good news in my case. My mom was a bit of a hippie. She claims to have been aware of the exact moment of my conception. She and my dad were celebrating completion of her thesis on the beastliness and beauty of Nabokov's fiction A little afternoon...um, seminar. Somewhere there in, *shazam*, the magic instant. She says she chose my name on the spot. *Ada,* Mr. Nabokov's last novel, the tale of incestuous twins, Ada and lover-brother, Van. Thankfully, I'm an only child."

"I imagine 'Lolita' might have been even more problematic," Frank noted with a mischievous grin.

Ada took another taste of her *mojito*. "I've always been a tad in awe of any character capable of inspiring the lines: *Light of my life, fire of my loins, my sin, my soul, Lolita.*"

"Well, a toast to fancy prose style, then."

"Here, here."

It was several anecdotes and another mojito later that Ada mentioned who had sent her. Hearing Peter's name, Frank allowed himself a brief, bright smile, then nodded. Ada, still unsure what specific knowledge Peter had sent her to glean from this man, started from the beginning. He listened patiently in silence until she held up the slip with his name on it and concluded, "so, here I am."

"Ada, it appears our mutual friend Peter has sent you to learn the origin of a legend. Would you be available for dinner?

"I have the feeling I'm not dressed right," she hesitated, looking down at her cords and loafers."

"Not to worry," we can swing by for you to change on the way.

EL TROPICANA

Brightly colored bulbs on a glittering sign illuminated the faces of patrons entering *El Tropicana*. Samba sounds surged as the doors swung open to reveal a crowd of dark-eyed men and dynamically-curved divas. Ada and Frank absorbed the undulation of the other guests, as their host led them across the grand dance floor to a table at the front.

After seeing Ada safely seated, the impeccably mannered maître d turned his attentions to Frank. "I trust you and the senorita will be comfortable here, Mr. Wayne. I'll have a bottle sent over immediately."

"Gracias, Armando."

With a smart bow, Armando slipped away, and Ada leaned forward, "Who could have imagined such a place existed...and in Arlington, Virginia. It's like something out the 1950's. I almost expect to see Carmen Miranda appear on stage." She straightened a bit, taking her elbows off the table, "I think it's so wonderful."

Frank smiled.

Ada settled back in her chair, enjoying the rustle of emerald green silk that accompanied her every movement. She was pleased that she'd gone for the most glamorous frock in her closet to match Frank, who had turned himself out in flawless white tie. Why shouldn't she finally make use of the gem she'd picked up in a San Francisco vintage shop? She'd descended the steps from her apartment building to Frank's idling roadster, happy that she'd been able to change, and curious to see what lay ahead.

Now, here they were. A striking, if somewhat unconventional pair.

Frank surveyed the surroundings. "I'm glad this spot makes an impression on you. I had begun to think today's youth as impervious to the allure of glamor," but, he added with a wink, "I did choose this spot for a special reason. There is no more perfect setting for our story within a thousand miles of here."

He lifted a flute of the champagne that they'd been served. "You see, there is indeed a very good explanation as to why Miguel Santos, Founder of Santos Fiesta Cruise Lines, would pour his money into politics. It has everything to do with the home of the original Tropicana nightclub, the island of Cuba.

Ada watched Frank take a long sip. "Have you ever heard reference to a man known as *the Bat*."

"Like Batman and Robin?" she puzzled.

Frank chuckled. "I'll take it from the top."

Ada nodded encouragement.

"The Miguel Santos you've begun to look into is known to some as "the Bat." *El Murcielago* in Spanish. The nickname refers to what has been reported as his daring escape from a Cuban prison in 1959. The jail break was, and still is, hailed as an amazing feat, a heroic triumph over Castro's communist repression."

"How did he get free?"

"Santos has consistently refused to divulge any of the details. This silence, of course, only adds to the mystery. Legends of Santaría spells and magical powers swirled around his tale of triumph. A bat, rising under cloak of darkness to rule the night skies, is how his admirers came to see him. Santos absolutely cultivated – perhaps even spread – the mystique. Thus, the *Murcielago* myth was born."

"Why was he jailed in the first place?" Ada asked.

"Rivalry, supposedly. Santos maintains that when they were both politically outspoken university students, Castro was jealous of Santos' charismatic appeal. The story repeated by Santos admirers is that Castro's paranoia grew even more pronounced after the revolution when Santos began to speak out for the old order of the Bautista regime. They say Castro accused Santos of an assassination plot and incarcerated him as an enemy of the state."

"Was it true?"

"The charges? The rivalry? The plot? That, dear Ada, is a matter of much dispute. Skeptics at the time, myself included, questioned the veracity of Santos' story. The supposed jail escape just didn't seem plausible and no one had even heard of the man before he showed up in Miami. But in the temperament of the late Fifties, doubts were ignored. It served too many people's ideological purposes. So, the unbelievable became the miraculous. Santos fit what the deposed elite wanted to believe. Inconsistencies were accepted as articles of faith. And now, the legend stands as gospel to its believers."

"If he started out as a revolutionary, then switched his allegiance to Bautista, perhaps the only truth is that he's a man without core values."

Frank nodded for her continue.

"He wouldn't be the first political opportunist. What does this have to do with the today though?"

"The Bat's influence has only grown with the years. His supporters see Santos as the embodiment of the exile's American Dream, immigrant turned millionaire. He's lauded as a community activist who has not forgotten his native roots – or the man who pulled them up. His stated mission is to vanquish Castro, return all expropriated property, and to lift up the poor on the rising tide of a return to capitalism."

"But surely he has his critics"?

"Santos is a Machiavellian fraud." Frank's face grew red. "He waves the flag of freedom to cloud selfish motives and dictatorial plans. He plots the demise of Castro not for the good of the Cuban people, but in order to have himself installed as Cuba's next leader."

Ada leaned back, hoping to quell his anger somewhat. After a moment, she said quietly: "He's a dangerous man."

"Very," Frank replied.

Ada was beginning to see new sides of the charming Franklin Aristotle Wayne. There was an edge of anger in his voice, a distant look in his eyes. Ada took a breath, then asked.

"Is there personal history here?"

Frank gave an ironic cough. "That, dear Ada, is a chapter too tedious to be told."

"I don't believe a word of that," she smiled. "Why don't we talk about how what you have told me fits into my research. Is Santos, the Bat or whatever, just trying to make friends in high places – setting up for when he's Havana's head honcho?"

"Yes, but his plans are more targeted than that. The means to Santos' end – his far-from-secret weapon – is the formidable Cuban American Liberation Bond (CALB). When you go back to check your notes, you'll see donations from CALB and its affiliates and associates largely map to those from Santos and his various tentacles. CALB or "the Cabal" as some call it, is a textbook illustration of how to win friends and influence people Washington-style. CALB is incorporated as a non-profit educational organization, which receives federal grant money to assist the Immigration Service in processing incoming refugees from Cuba. It has an affiliate political action committee that hands out big bucks to sympathetic ears in Government, as does his corporate PAC. All this has helped Santos secure appointment to a new Presidential Advisory Commission on fostering democratic change in Cuba. He's deep in the rigging."

"I did see CALB in the FEC filings."

"Without a doubt, you'll find more than that, Ada. Though you may only guess it from their surnames, you'll also see hundreds of CALB members and their relatives, as well as donations from Fiesta Cruise Lines employees. Regular folks are often used to get around campaign contribution limits. Santos and other higher ups pass out envelopes of cash to reimburse their minions for political checks they're instructed to write."

"So, Santos gets around giving limits, but still gets credit for gathering the donations."

"He bundles the checks. Everyone knows CALB is Santos' brainchild. He maintains a certain paper distance from the Cabal's operations. Nevertheless, he is very firmly at the helm. He installed his nitwit half-brother as President, but the man is just a stooge primed to do Santos' bidding. The whole CALB network is so devoted to Santos and his mission that he has only to make his wishes known and they are pursued with almost religious devotion."

"Thomas a' Becket."

"Precisely. Every casual comment executed as a command.'"

"He sounds a perfect puppet-maker."

"That," Frank declared, "and a ruthless schemer. Whether or not Castro really threw him in the clink, I know I would have. But" he added, "I'd have made damn certain he never got out."

They both sat back. Their dinner had been cleared away. Glossy dishes of *flan* quivered expectantly alongside sweet-bitter cups of *Cafe' Cubano*. The Band began to play.

"Merengue?"

"No thank you. The flan is delicious," Ada dug her spoon in again.

Frank chuckled softly to himself and waited for her to finish dessert.

"Good?

"Mmmm."

"Ada?"

"Frank. You may now have this dance."

PLAY IT AGAIN

Monday morning. As traffic on the Beltway stalled the progress of some commuters, a jam outside the door of COG's intern pit delayed others. The hallway was being blocked by a procedural demonstration. Meringue 101.

"Okay, now step like you're edging sideways down an aisle at a movie theater, shift the hips back and forth, back and forth, back and forth."

"Can we take it from the top again?" came a plea from the crowd.

"Sure thing." Ada set her coffee cup down for safety's sake. "Right then. Mark the beat. Think: 'excuse me, excuse me' with each swing-shift. That's better; move it like you mean it."

Whoops went up as the whole room transformed into a parade of pelvic metronomes, ticking away in raucous concert: "excuse me, excuse me, excuse me...."

"EXCUSE ME," interjected a voice out of sync with the others. All heads swung towards Peter's secretary, Rosie. The circle closed around her and Rosie picked up the beat, as she inched towards Ada. "Honey, I think you'll need to sit the next one out," she called. "Peter's in his office, pacing. I get the feeling he's waiting to talk to you. Run along upstairs and see what's on his mind."

"Right-O, Rosie," Ada called back, retrieving her java and making for the door, calling over her shoulder, "I'll be back for the bossa nova!"

Peter's back was to the door as she entered. He was staring out the window, listening to someone on the other end of the phone. Ada seated herself in the chair farthest from his desk. It was the only empty one. The others were fully loaded with books, files, and everything from a squash racket to a doll with the face of Oliver North and the body of Pee Wee Herman. From the looks of things, Peter had spent the remainder of his weekend in the office. The clutter hadn't been reduced since she'd left him on Saturday, but it had definitely been rearranged. Another thing she noticed, and supposed had previously been blocked from view, was a beautifully carved war club hung alongside a brilliant head-dress of interlaced feathers and beads. She'd just begun to ponder this, when she heard him ring off.

"Hey. Looks like you've done some excavating."

"Yeah, just trying to straighten things up." Grinning, "Needed to make some space since I have an office mate now." They both scanned the room, two sets of eyes taking in the inescapable fact that chaos still predominated. "Okay, I know what you're thinking" he said, "reshuffling chairs on the Titanic."

Ada smiled. "No, great. Thanks for trying. It's looking good!" Peter gave her a skeptical look. She laughed: "And, hey, you've uncovered buried treasure. She pointed: "Kayapo Indian?"

"A gift from Frank. He's taught you well. I gather you're now well-acquainted."

Ada nodded.

"Well. What did we learn?"

Dance lessons popped into her mind.

Peter countered with knowing wink: "He's an oracle."

"A teller of winds both foul and fair."

"The flight of the Bat."

"Yes, *Murcielago*. Flees dark jail cells without a trace. Soars to freedom, fame, and fortune in a single bound. Now spreading his mythical wings even wider."

Peter rubbed his hands together. "You're starting to sound like him."

"Too much dramatic dialogue?" she parried.

"Putting you two together puts a lot in play."

Ada wasn't certain what to say in response to his more serious tone.

Peter had turned to the window. He tapped out a rhythm on his knee.

"Peter?"

He turned around to face her and spoke quickly: "Miguel Santos seems to have something big up his sleeve. He's been working towards it for a long while." Peter stopped to tap off a few more thumps. "The sharp increase in campaign contributions, more aggressive activism. He's ramping up for something, preparing to call in bets."

"What do you think he's planning?" Ada asked, "He talks about wanting to rescue his people from the yoke of communism; but isn't it just...you know...talk. A publicity platform? Maybe he just rails against Castro to keep himself relevant. I mean, he can't seriously think the United States would invade Cuba and hand it over to him." She could almost now identify the tune of the tapping. "Does he?"

"He may think he can capture the prize by other means. As I'm sure Frank explained, this is a man obsessed with the power and misdirection is a game he's studied from the inside out."

Rosie poked her head in to remind him of his next meeting. Holding up the representative number of fingers, "They'll be up in two minutes, Peter." Throwing Ada a wink, "But take a couple extra, honey. I'll keep 'em at bay."

"Spoils me," Peter shook his head. *Tap Ta-Tap Tap.* "Where was I?" *Snap* "Oh, so stop me if Frank covered this." She nodded for him to continue. "At university, Santos flirted with revolutionary ideas. He wore rakish berets, quoted Che Guevarra and ranted about government corruption and subservience to Yanqui interests. No one bought it. He was the son of a wealthy businessman with thinly disguised ties to American mobsters. Most saw him as either a buffoon or cynical manipulator. If his fellow students didn't dismiss him outright, they avoided him, or occasionally humored his posturing in exchange for free drinks. But even those desperate few usually couldn't stomach his rhetoric for more than one round. Santos parroted the talk of the time, but it rang hollow and he had no followers."

"Wait, if that was the case, why would Castro have bothered locking him up?"

"That's Frank's big question mark. Must be more to it than Santos' implausible story of rivalry and spite."

"Maybe Fidel just decided it'd be a public service to have Santos incarcerated as a general nuisance."

"Perhaps..." *Tap Tap T-Tap-Tap.* "In any case, whatever happen before he fled the island, by the time Santos arrived in the United States, he was fully pro-Bautista and treated as a hero, a martyr, and a patron saint of the newly-deposed. The wealthy exiles in Miami welcomed him as a prodigal son. He was a son of one of their own, after all. It didn't take long for them to put him in touch with the U.S. intelligence operatives plotting to take down Castro. Operation Mongoose, as it was called, relied heavily on Cuban-American recruits to carry out its often harebrained schemes."

"The assassination attempts?"

"The catalogue is extensive." Peter yelled out into the hallway, "Rosie, five more minutes." He leaned back with his hands behind his head. "One idea was to dust Castro's shoes with thallium salts to cause his beard to fall out, hence negating his most charismatic attribute. There was also a plot to poison Castro's cigars with lethal botulism. And, before that, a plan to lace his cigars with a disorienting drug, so that when he gave a speech, people would think he was too stoned to govern. Santos has been linked to any number of these failed efforts, as well as to the biggest dud, the Bay of Pigs fiasco."

"You and Frank have both mentioned connections to underground figures," Ada interposed.

"The syndicate conspired with both the CIA and the exile community. They forged an unholy Trinity on a mission of retribution. You see, the mob felt twice betrayed by Fidel. The North American Mafia considered Batista their man, but to hedge their bets, they ran some guns for Castro in the mid-Fifties. When Castro's revolution swept into Havana, however, instead of thanking them for the weapons and ammo, he shut the mob down and kicked them out. The closing of the casinos, bordellos, and drug operations cost bosses like Meyer Lansky dearly. Lansky reportedly put out a million-dollar contract for Castro's head. Since that's just what the CIA and the exiles had in mind, the three sides joined forces."

Peter took a deep breath and exhaled slowly. "I could go on, but my point is that Santos is now well-schooled in the art of underhanded intrigue. It's become his operational trademark. He likes to fight his battles in the shadows. He keeps his troops in civilian clothing.

"The Cuban American Liberation Bond?"

"Right. 'The Cabal' functions as his foot soldiers. CALB's individual members and its political action committee have contributed millions of dollars to finance elections. This largess wins the deep appreciation of key politicians and the party machines. Doesn't matter who is in the White House, Santos has a standing invitation. When Santos lobbies U.S. officials to intensify the embargo against Castro, humanitarian objections, international law, and protests from the rest of the business community are all but ignored. What's more, when CALB's non-profit branch applies for federal grants to do anything from refugee processing to "democracy building," they receive more than favorable consideration. Even a project as fatuous as designing hand-held video games with villainous Castros being chased by heroic Uncle Sams gets funded."

Incredulous, Ada interjected, "The U.S. government pays for video games?"

"Oh, yeah. The plan was to airlift 200,000 of these video players and drop them over the island to masses of Cuban youths below. Tragically, not one of these electronic infiltrators survived the mission. It seems their little parachutes failed to open on descent. The skies over Havana rained microchips and metal that day. The fallout of this was two-fold: 1) Castro used the recovered circuitry to repair old Soviet-era short-wave radios, and 2) hard-liners in Congress accused the Mexican parachute manufacturer of sabotage and raised the import duties on their products by 500 percent."

"So sad it's funny." She sighed. "Peter, if you already knew so much about Santos and the Cabal, why did you send me to Frank?"

"Didn't you enjoy meeting him?"

"You know I did."

"I do know."

Rosie called out. "Your five minutes are up, Peter."

She'd begun standing to leave, but he held her arm. "Ada, Frank really does know more about Santos and how he operates than anyone else, so if this turns into something, it'll be helpful to have him involved." Ada nodded. "But I guess the truth is that Frank Wayne is very dear to me. He's a great man who's had some tough breaks, most of which can be blamed on Miguel Santos. I can't get into the whole history now; but, bringing Frank in on our project is my way of making him...well, I'm not sure how to put it...."

"I understand," said Ada.

Peter held her a second longer, nodded, then moved his hand to a pile of papers on his desk.

Chapter 3

FALL 1958

The young man had served the State Department long enough to recognize a run-around. He'd been locked in a diplomatic two-step by the pinstriped brigade for weeks now. He knew how to whistle their tune and follow their lead; but this time, he couldn't continue to play their game. The stakes were too high.

With each new day of delay, mutiny grew in his mind, anxiety in his heart. He needed to get back in. He needed to get her out.

The situation is sticky, they would say, prevaricating. Damn right, he'd reply. I ought to know. Wasn't I the desk officer who'd sent umpteen cables to that effect (and apparently, to no avail) for months? Great time to wise up, fellows. It may be too late to save your puppet, but there's still time to save her. I have to get back. To hell with official travel papers. I'll swim there, if that's what it takes.

A knock at the door interrupted his rumination. "Sir, this arrived in the overnight pouch. We're not sure how it got in, but..."

"Hand it here."

OCTOPI

Ada had always loved the journey to and from Quinn's family estate in Great Falls, Virginia. She especially savored the drive home through soaring trees and granite boulders, then along the bridge-ribbed Potomac. This evening, however, she was distracted. When she failed to remark, as per her custom, at the twinkling lights of the boathouses, Quinn steered off the parkway and towards Martin's Tavern.

"Okay, spill," he insisted once they were seated knee-to-knee on adjoining barstools.

"I guess I gave myself away," she said with a soft smile.

"You always applaud that spot. What's up?"

"I'm overreacting," she shrugged, spinning her Guinness on its coaster. Ada sneaked a glance and saw Quinn eyeing her skeptically. She took a long pull.

"Your father said something tonight that... well it made me feel odd."

Quinn shook his head, "Ada, if you going to tell me my dad propositioned you..."

"Oh, God, Quinn, don't be ridiculous. No, he warned me. When you were out tending the grill, I started telling him about my project at COG. He got very serious; you know that stern stare, ponderous frown thing he does. Then he said: 'Be careful, Ada, don't look into holes when you don't know what's on the other side.'"

"Well," Quinn sat back and stretched his arms out, "he does like to lecture against independence of thought."

"Yeah. I told you I was overreacting," she said, quickly adding, "it's just that these stories about covert plots and shady deals. I dunno, it makes me feel as though I'm entering another world." Ada paused. "It's like I'm circling a web of intrigue and it's only a matter of time before I get pulled in."

"Beware the lure of the octopus, Ada. If you listen to too many conspiracy theories, you'll start suspecting your own reflection is a double agent."

"You're right," she said brightly. Quinn always knew how to settle her down, even if that often entailed letting the wind out of her sails. In this case, she was grateful.

They went on to speak of other things. Pints drained, they left. Quinn held her hand. The evening had grown cool. Wind gusts quickened their steps; Quinn tightened his grip. Once inside the car, they waited in silence for the engine to warm up. Ada struggled with her seatbelt, trying with too cold fingers to slide it into place. The troublesome mechanism finally engaged with a resolute *click*.

"Quinn," she began tentatively, "don't you ever wonder when you hear stories about the other side of history?"

Poking her playfully, "Such as?"

"Tonkin Gulf, Watergate, detonating cigars, arms for hostages. Aren't you ever amazed?"

"Amazed that it happened or that people found out?"

"We doubt the absurd or the inconceivable, yet it seems to happen again and again, right under our noses."

BUSY BEES

Satellite structures flank the U.S. Capitol Building. The three on the northern side – Dirksen, Hart and Russell – accommodate Senators and their staff. The three to the south serve the personages and personnel of "the other body," the House of Representatives. The most modern of these lower chamber buildings is a gargantuan structure named for a famous Texan, the inimitable former Speaker of the House Sam Rayburn. By the time its construction was completed in 1965, the working monument had cost taxpayers over $100 million. It was the most expensive government structure ever built at the time, with higher price tab even than the Pentagon.

If an edifice is supposed to reflect the characteristics of its namesake, this one is appropriately overwhelming, but lacks the personality of the original. Its marbled halls offer sterility rather than Rayburnian warmth. Nonetheless, the Rayburn Building is considered the most desirable of the three House locales because its offices usually offer an extra 10 square-feet of floor space. This is no small issue considering most rooms have to accommodate at least six staffers, their desks, files, and dreams of greatness.

Jaime worked in the Rayburn building. He still got a kick out of flashing his I.D. badge to the guards when entering. It gave him the sense that he'd finally arrived. He wasn't alone. All over town, you'd spot those bits of plastic dangling after office hours like dog tags, medals from an undeclared war.

Jaime had just emerged from his Monday morning legislative staff meeting. He thumped his chest, rattling loose the tension between his ribs. This tightness he'd come to consider normal. Nervous excitement, he craved it like a drug. Someday, he figured, the adrenaline rush of panic and pressure would lose its potency. For now, he'd ride it.

Jaime picked up a pile of messages on his way through the reception area and settled in at his desk. Full plate again this week. He made a list so formal that it suggested he hoped for posterity.

To do:

- Prep for Committee mark-up of Foreign Assistance Act. Send draft amendments to Leg. Counsel. Touch base with committee staff. Give State/White House a heads-up. Write talking points and amendment summaries for circulation. Work with Mark on press strategy.
- Draft floor statement on resolution disapproving the choice by former Yugoslavian republic of "Macedonia" as its new name. Call local Greek-American club in N.J.
- Draft letter to President regarding normalization of relations with Vietnam.
- Write speech for weekend rally in Miami. Get more info on program agenda and attendees. Check on tickets & hotel.

In addition to these tasks, Jaime would be called upon to respond, both in writing and on the phone, to disgruntled constituents in the Honorable Richard Peralta's New Jersey district. Everything crossed his transom, from problems with the surface quality of federal toll roads to allegations that the CIA was practicing mind control by imbedding microchips in the brains of US mail carriers. Like many congressional staffers, Jaime's portfolio was comprehensive. He handled issue areas far beyond his scope of expertise, including: all matters related to Banking, Commerce, Justice, Veterans, the Office of Management and Budget, and the Transportation Department. Each day had its high and low points. From helping his boss protect vital American interests to making voters feel heard. Either way, it's public service, he reminded himself. Oh yeah, and getting his boss reelected. That was the unofficial part of the job.

Jaime's intercom buzzed and the Congressman's executive assistant announced the arrival of his 10 a.m. appointment: "Mr. Cortina and guests have arrived."

"Thanks, Ruth. Please show them into Rick's office and say I'll be right there." Jaime grabbed a couple of business cards and his notebook and headed towards the Congressman's office. Since the Hon. Richard Peralta had been called to the floor for a vote, Jaime would be free to use his more spacious quarters for the meeting.

Jaime entered the room to be embraced immediately. Tito Cortina, President of the Cuban American Liberation Bond, was a jovial man with a habit of patting people frequently on the back and maintaining a rumbling chuckle throughout even the most sensitive of conversations. This was their first encounter.

"Tito Cortina. Call me Tito. Even my brother calls me Tito!"

Jaime noticed he bared his teeth when he smiled.

"That's a little joke, my friend," Tito added, nudging one of the other guests to ensure his humor was appreciated.

Tito had brought three of his underlings at CALB with him to meet Jaime, Rick's bright new legislative aide. The monologue went something like this: Tito felt sure they would have a wonderful time working together on the critical goal of saving the people of Cuba. Rick Peralta was a hero. Jaime should know how deeply he, Tito, respected the good congressman. Tito suggested they all gather for a drink soon to toast the forces of freedom and justice. Jaime politely declined this invitation in the short-term, citing his need to help prepare for the big rally in Miami, which CALB was sponsoring.

Of course, the rally, Tito laughed heartily, how could he forget. Had Jaime received his event tickets? Was all in order? Ah, splendid. Well, they would have many opportunities to celebrate on that special occasion. Jaime would be very moved by some of the stories he would hear at the rally. CALB, which has for years been instrumental in helping resettle refugees fleeing the devilish clutches of Fidel had rescued just two days ago a dozen members of Castro's elite military force. These freedom seekers had escaped by taking to the waters in inner tubes. Yes, a CALB vessel patrolling the perimeter of the island picked them up on radar. Just another example of how Rick Peralta – chief sponsor of the

Immigration & Naturalization Service grant program which funds this private refugee rescue and relief effort, has helped the cause.

Truly amazing, Jaime agreed. He assured Tito he was very much looking forward to the weekend. He knew as well that the Congressman felt honored to be among the invited speakers. It would be a historic event. It's certainly a time of great change for the island and Jaime said he would be interested to hear of conditions first-hand from these recent arrivals. Until then. Thank you all for coming by. Tito, it's a pleasure to meet you. Take care. Yes, we'll see you on Friday.

Back slap. *Mucho gusto. Hasta luego.*

HAWK AND DOVE

It hadn't been easy for Ada to convince her busy friend to meet for lunch, but Jaime found he could never say no to her. Anyway, he reasoned, the short walk down Independence Avenue to the Hawk 'n Dove would fortify him for the long day ahead.

Ada was craving fortification too. She was hungry for more information on Santos and insight into how CALB operated on the Hill. Ada was pleased to think she already had "connections" to tap for inside intelligence. I'm entering the Rolodex race, she mused, where the winners are the ones who could get facts the fastest. What better source could she have asked for than her old buddy, Jaime, who was practically writing key parts of the legislation she was interested in. So, let's do lunch, she reasoned.

The Hawk 'n Dove was relatively full, but Jaime spotted Ada at a table near the bar beneath a large picture of Richard Nixon shaking hands with Elvis Presly. The median age of the crowd was twenty-something. It was mostly Hill staffers, interns, and lower-rung associates of organizations headquartered near the Capitol. Lobbyists dined at expensive restaurants like Le Mistral when seeking to impress a client, an underfed aide, or simply to exercise an expense account. The plebs were left happily alone to enjoy the reliably cheap and greasy fare at the Hawk 'n Dove.

"Cheeseburger medium-well and a BLT no mayo for the lady, please. One coke, one iced tea, and two waters."

"Comin' right up, sir."

Ada had the good manners not to plunge right in. It's never polite to pump even good friends for gossip without a little warm up.

"How's your week going? New job still great?"

"Awesome," Jaime leaned back. "I mean, some stuff is a drag. Like responding to constituent mail. I get sometimes 200 letters a week and even robot responses take time. But mostly I love it. I never realized how much room a Member of Congress can make for themselves on a particular issue."

Ada raised an eyebrow and tilted her head in listening mode.

"The legislature is totally the loose cannon branch of government. We can just charge ahead with full guns blazing and the White House, State, and everyone has to pay attention because we hold the purse strings. We're where the rubber hits the road. And, you know, we really can make a difference."

"Tell me more," Ada urged as the food arrived.

"Well, take this morning for one. I had this truly inspiring meeting. These guys, they're exiles from Cuba, right, but they haven't just come to America to make a buck and forget the past, they're actually sailing out to sea to rescue countrymen trying to make it in America. They have a whole plan for a new democratic government in Cuba. Once Castro is gone, they can just move in and get things rolling again...investments, infrastructure, development assistance...they've got it in the bag. No awkward transition period, no internal confusion, just a smooth segue back to peace and prosperity."

Back to peace and prosperity? Ada tried not to roll her eyes. But this was the intel she'd come for, so she just nodded.

Jaime went on to tell her about the upcoming weekend in Miami. His first official trip. "It's not just a junket. I'm furthering critical national interests and all."

Okay, let's mellow out here for minute, she warned herself. Ada waited for the waitress to finish refilling their water glasses, then asked, "Jaime, are these people affiliated with the Cuban American Liberation Bond?"

"They *are* the Cuban American Liberation Bond," he said with some surprise. "Are you getting into foreign policy over there at COG? I thought the focus was mostly corporate welfare and pork barrel spending."

Ada tried to sound casual. "I'm trying to school up on all the influential groups to figure out who is who and what is what."

How the hell did I get myself into this, she thought to herself. And what do I do now? The memory of an FEC list floated up from her subconscious and the name Richard Peralta. How could I have been so stupid? Why didn't the simple fact that Jaime might work for a Santos supporter not register in her dim little brain? What a complete fool. This is not how lunch was supposed to go. *Damn,* she muttered.

"Damn what?" Jaime asked, forking a heap of French fries from her plate.

She watched her friend swirling the pile around in a pool of ketchup. "Have the rest if you like," she offered, pushing her lunch towards him. Should she say something about the COG investigation? How would Jaime react? Would Peter object? Do friendships survive professional disagreements? What would Warren Christopher advise? Oh, never mind! It's a fine mess, that's the only sure conclusion, she decided.

"How's the crew. Seen anyone?" Jaime asked between mouthfuls.

"Not lately. Well, Quinn. We had dinner out at his dad's place."

"China and crystal deal?"

"No, thankfully. Mrs. Keegan was away in Palm Springs, so it was just the three of us. We grilled and ate on the terrace like savages!"

"Yeah, right! And how is the good Senator?"

"The same. Pressing Quinn about his future. Golden opportunities. Waste of talent and all that. You know the tune."

"Yeah, I've heard it a time or two. What about Quinn then? He at least seems to have no regrets. He likes his muckraking gig well enough, right? Does he tell you anything about it?"

"I think he's enjoying himself. But you know," Ada shrugged, "it could just be the novelty factor. Not sure how long he'll stick with it. The challenge may fade in time."

"Yes, well, that's a chronic issue for our boy, isn't it?" Jaime seemed to catch himself, adding, "Except where you're concerned."

Under normal circumstances, Ada would have responded to such a comment with either gentle derision or wicked humor. In her flustered state, however, honesty hopped the hurdles. "Maybe our star is not dimmed, just evolved. I guess my feelings have changed some too. It's hard to keep renewing the mystery when we're just so much alike. Sometimes I think we're more siblings than a pair of consenting adults. The curse of two only children, perhaps."

Jaime laughed, "I love twins! Aren't you named for one?"

She shook a scolding finger at him, "Ha. Let's leave naughty Mr. Nabokov out of this."

The adjacent table leaned in hoping for more details and Jaime pretended to doodle on his napkin suggestively. Ada relaxed some, and perhaps buoyed by this jocularity, resolved to return to the uncomfortable subject.

"So, Miami," she tested, "that's really exciting. Will you be busy with events the whole time? I mean, what level of participation is required? No doubt tanning yourself and mingling with the locals is mandatory."

"Work and play, my friend, is a cocktail I'm always pleased to sample."

"I wish you luck in all your ventures, Jaime," she joked.

They chatted a bit longer about nothing in particular, until Ada noticed the waiter lurking with the bill in hand. With their account settled, the two friends made their way out into the bright slanting glare.

Squinting, "I'm glad you could make lunch. Gives me a chance to wish you bon voyage." She gave him a hug and joked, "Bring me a souvenir? Just some sand or a swizzle stick to remind me of my wilder days."

"Anything to usher them back," Jaime countered. "Hey, let's do this again when I return. I can fill you in on the trip. Maybe we can get Quinn and some of the others to join."

"Sure, that sounds nice."

With a wave good-bye, they headed in opposite directions.

PORCUPINE'S GOOD POINTS

Hands on hips, Rosie stood in the doorway. "You've been in a mood since you got back from lunch. What's got your hackles up?"

"I'm sorry," Ada sighed.

"Why so down?" Rosie cast a motherly smile, "You should be flying high. Life's going well."

"Oh Rosie, you're right. I just had a weird thing happened, and I was hoping Peter would be back this afternoon, so I could fill him in. I can't seem to focus." Ada dropped into a chair.

Rosie took the seat beside her. "Look honey, you don't need to apologize. I'm here to listen. You think Peter keeps me around for my typing? Ha! We all need folks to listen when we weep. You come to Rosie, when you need a shoulder."

Ada looked up, "I feel better already." Her grey eyes cleared. "I suppose there's no urgency in talking to Peter anyhow."

Rosie patted Ada's hand as she rose, "hold on a sec." Rosie went out to her desk and returned with several files wrapped together with a band. "Peter certainly thinks he needs this stuff pretty urgently. Called me on his way over to a Senate hearing before I came to check on you. He asked me to bring these by his house this evening, to save him coming back to the office. Normally it'd be no problem. But my grandson has this school pageant tonight and Peter lives all the way over in northwest..."

"Maybe I could help."

"Oh, honey, would you?' Rosie added a little too quickly, he lives on U Street – 14th and U."

"No prob. That's only a metro stop from my place. What time were you supposed to go by?" Ada asked.

"He thought he'd be home by seven-thirty. Is that too late?"

"I have plenty to keep me busy until then, especially now that you've got me back in productive work mode."

"Like I say, anytime. Anytime, Ada, you just come to Rosie." She jotted down Peter's address. "Thanks for the favor."

"No, thank you. It gives me a chance..." Ada paused. "Ah, I get it." Ada embraced her.

"Ooo, all right, that's enough. Run along now, I got things to do."

"Bless you, Rosie," Ada called out as she sat back down.

BACK IN TERRAPIN

President Woodrow Wilson comes off quite well in high school history books for his post-war principles of peace and faith in a League of Nations. Back on the home front, however, Wilson promoted the KKK and sought to segregate the federal workforce. This reversed decades of post-Reconstruction progress for African Americans, particularly in the District of Columbia. By the 1920s and 1930s, economic access was returning, and Black culture began to thrive again in the nation's capital. At the center of this resurgence was the U Street corridor. Known as the Black Broadway, the area was home to hundreds of nightclubs, which showcased the likes of Nat King Cole, Duke Ellington, and Pearl Bailey. Grand hotels, glamorous theaters and rows of beautiful houses, designed by black architects and backed by black financiers, made it a mecca. Black academics, businessmen, doctors and entertainers all numbered among the community's favorite sons and daughters.

Then, mid-century, everything seemed to unravel anew. Ironically, desegregation was a driver of the neighborhood's demise, as blacks moved to the suburbs. The final blow came in 1968, when riots following the assassination of Martin Luther King Jr., left the community decimated. For the next two decades, the once vibrant corridor remained home to burned-out buildings, and crumbling storefronts, painful reminders of a dream unmet. Things eventually began to turn around at the tail end of the '80s, when revitalization became a catch phrase of urban renewal. Savvy real estate developers, along with small business owners and young professionals started to move in. Building by building, block by block, sections of the U Street Corridor came back to life.

Peter had bought his place without knowing much about the neighborhood. He stumbled upon it by mistake on a long walk. The faded "for sale" sign whistled with story. He'd felt at home and moved in before the hipsters arrived in earnest.

Ada's apartment on Connecticut Avenue was only 10 minutes up the road, but this was her first time venturing down U Street. When she exited the metro station that evening at half-past seven, she searched for clues on which way to go. She often lost her bearings when underground. Rather than appeal to one of the preoccupied commuters brushing past her, Ada took a guess, turned right and began to walk. The autumn sky had grown dark. She quickened her pace and cursed herself for not checking the kiosk map. A street sign finally appeared to tell her she'd overshot her mark by a block. Ada spun around to reverse course and, in doing so, ran smack into a large bearded man, knocking his hat to the ground. Startled and embarrassed, Ada bent down to retrieve it. She noticed the man wore plastic gloves. Bizarre, she thought, the kind that doctors used for hygiene not warmth. She was about to launch into an apology, when the man snatched his hat away, and without comment, hurried off in the direction from which he'd come. Ada stood for a moment looking after him, then shook herself back into gear. "Great," she muttered to herself, "nice meeting you too."

She'd pushed the incident out of her mind by the time she arrived at Peter's door. Staring up at the narrow two-story stone house with its turreted windows, she thought it more whimsical a place than she'd imagined would suit Peter Vane. She could see lights upstairs and a faint glow coming from the back of the house. There was no doorbell, so she knocked and waited. Music seemed to be playing. She knocked again. Still no answer. Ada craned to peer through the semi-circular pane above the door and detected no signs of movement. She figured her knocks were getting swallowed by the stereo, and likely couldn't reach him on the upper level. She decided to hang out and wait for a shadow to indicate he'd come down the stairs. As she sat down to wait, the wind carried the music to her in waves, bits and pieces of a ballad:

winds both foul and fair all swarm…

many years ago…

came through many fights but lost at love…

An arc of light expanded across the entryway and Ada looked up with an absent expression to see a tall haloed form. Her eyes adjusted and there was Peter with his hand outstretched. "Let me help you up."

She blinked.

"Have you been waiting long?" he asked.

"No, I don't think so. I knocked," she explained, smiling with more assurance now, "but I think *Lady with the Fan* drowned me out."

"Busted," Peter laughed. "Come on in." He led her past the entry hall and into the kitchen, remarking as he did, "it's an old end-of-day habit: Grateful Dead at high decibels." He handed her a beer from the 'fridge and pulled out a chair for her to sit on. He leaned against the counter and took a steady pull from his bottle. Fixing her with a curious look, "you like?"

Ada hesitated, momentarily unsure whether he was referring to the choice of music or brand of beverage. Deciding it didn't matter, "Absolutely," she replied.

Peter met her smile. He took another sip. Ada watched him unwind. It began with a gradual loosening around the jawline, then the shoulders rounded ever so slightly, the hips tipped a minuscule amount, and when the last remnants of the long day were ready to be banished from within, he began taping his foot against the wood floor. Peter looked down as though at some foreign creature.

"Another old habit," he said planting his foot firmly and straightening. "Come on, let me give you a tour."

A coin dropped in the back of her mind. *That's* the tune he was tapping the other day. An invocation of the muse that begins the Terrapin song suite. Its slow cadence. *In token rhyme, suggesting rhythm.*

They'd been through every room in the house before Ada realized that she was still carrying the banded stack of files from Rosie. He had yet to ask her reason for coming. Peter's house was peaceful, inviting. Ada found herself wanting to spend more time exploring the various knickknacks, mementos, books, and boxes scattered throughout. He seemed to have much more stuff than she expected from someone still in his late twenties or early thirties. Maybe he just hung onto more things than the other men she'd known. Is sentimentality a female trait? Maybe one day, I'll stop analyzing so much, she sighed silently to herself.

They had arrived in the living room. Peter returned to the kitchen to fetch two more beers. When he came back, Ada pointed to Rosie's files, "I offered to deliver them. I hope I haven't taken up too much of your evening with the tour and all."

"I haven't walked through my own house in weeks. It's nice to see the place again," he grinned, adding: "I like the company too. You're welcome anytime."

Ada, who'd actually come with a mind to talk about the day's events suddenly lost interest in seeking Peter's advice on business matters. Her distress over the lunch with Jaime had faded away and she didn't particularly want to talk about rich expatriates. She was interested in learning more about the man who, for lack of a better title, was her first real boss.

"What other music do you listen to?"

"Vinyl is over there. Play what you like," Peter offered. "Have you eaten? How about I cook?"

FLAMINGO ROAD

It wasn't until her gums started throbbing that our heroine realized she'd been brushing her teeth far longer than recommended. She spat the last stalwart bubbles of toothpaste into the sink. Mopping her face with the towel, Ada met her own reproachful reflection in the mirror. "Oh hell," she said aloud. "I need to nip this notion before it buds."

Brrrrrinnnggggg. Brrrrrinnnngggg. Ada cursed the toe she'd stubbed on route to the phone, answering impatiently, "Hello?"

"Ada. It's Peter. I figured you'd be home by now."

"Yep," she took a calming breath, "safe and sound. It's a short walk, you know. Yep, sure is." She was cataloging the various possible reasons for his call. For none of them would 'yep' be a particularly cogent refrain. Christ, she thought, he's talking again. Pay attention.

"... a great hook. We could use the Miami rally as the backdrop. It makes the report newsworthy, so we could get good coverage. What do you say?"

"The Miami rally?" she repeated, stalling to catch up.

"I know it puts us in a time crunch, but I just got word. CALB's flying a bunch of friendly Congressmen down to South Florida for a chest thumping spectacle. They'll rope off *Calle Ocho* and blast their speeches. It's the perfect backdrop for us to call them out on their full agenda."

Clued in at last. "So, we'd do a press conference or something around the....but" she paused, "there is no report."

"We have until mid-day Friday. That gives us 36 hours. All you need to do is tie what you've gleaned from finance records to CALB's legislative agenda. Didn't you have a friend you thought could give you a run down on what's on the docket at the Foreign Affairs Committee?"

"It's a long story, but I'm not sure that source will work."

"Don't worry," Peter interjected, "call Adam Stevens at the Library of Congress Congressional Research Division. Rosie will have the number. Most draft amendments flow through him; he'll have the heads up on the full sweep."

"Awesome."

"Call Adam first thing tomorrow. Then, let's you and I outline the report structure. Be in the office by 8."

"Okay."

"Ada."

"Yep."

"Imagine you're cramming for a term paper. No biggie. It'll be fine. Trust me."

Laughing, "I do. And that helps. Thanks. I'll see you at 8."

"Yep."

"Goodnight."

She put the phone down slowly. Her head was spinning with the realization of what she had to do between now and noon Friday. Ada got into bed and turned out the bedside light. She pulled the covers around her chin and watched shadows form on the ceiling.

Chapter 4

WINTER 1958

He used to call me "Caro." Indeed, she thought. In Spanish, the word meant "costly." Worth everything, he'd said. Now, the bitter irony. She had been forced to break his heart. To save his life. That was the price. She'd been given no choice. She would do as commanded. She would die inside so that he might live. She wrote the letter. "Do not come for me. I have found someone else. Good-bye."

LITTLE HAVANA

In 1849, the U.S. Army built a frontier settlement at the mouth of the Miami River. This kept the Seminole Indians at bay and later formed an outpost for commerce and rail lines. Hotels followed, but the City of Miami didn't really come into its own until the 1960s, when hundreds of thousands of Cubans fleeing Fidel Castro's government arrived. Unlike other American immigrants who sought to assimilate in their newfound land, this boon of exiles replanted Cuban culture on American soil. The climate and flora matched perfectly, so why not rebuild the life that had been expropriated. Architecture, entertainment, and enterprise was simply grafted onto a new rootstock. The capitol of this expat Eden was Little Havana.

Visitors to this neighborhood and its main strip, *Calle Ocho*, encounter visions of an age gone by. Ubiquitous sidewalk coffee strands, old men playing dominos and smoking cigars, women gossiping in clustered groups, kids selling coconuts – were all reminiscent of a time when dashing men drove glamorous divas along the Malecón.

Jaime marveled as he wound his way to CALB's Miami offices. He had asked the cab driver to drop him off a few blocks shy of his intended destination. With a half-hour to kill, he wanted to catch the buzz of street energy and double it with a syrupy jolt of *cafe cubano*.

Jaime's boss Rick Peralta had flown in earlier for a fundraiser luncheon in his honor, hosted by the Cabal. As an employee of the

American Taxpayer, the size of his boss' campaign kitty wasn't supposed to concern or involve Jaime, though of course it did. Jaime had written a short address for Rick to deliver and prepped him on various questions that he might get asked by the lunch-goers. However, to avoid the appearance of impropriety, Jaime did not attend in person. Nor would he be physically present at any of the other events CALB had scheduled for the purposes of showering its congressional supporters with financial appreciation. Not to worry, though, there were plenty of other events on the weekend's itinerary for Jaime to attend. One such was the meeting just getting underway in CALB's executive conference room.

Upon entering the room, Jaime spotted his boss. He also recognized Tito Cortina. But the figure that drew his attention was that of a man he knew only from news clippings: Miguel Santos, patriot, hero, and the one that they call "the Bat."

Rick Peralta came towards Jaime with his hand extended.

"Welcome to Little Havana!"

"Sir, hi. How was the lunch?"

"Very successful!" Rick Peralta slapped a hand on Jaime's shoulder, "one for the record books."

"Fantastic. Are you all set for tomorrow?"

"I read your draft on the plane...great speech." Rick guided him through the crowd, "come, I want to introduce you."

Moments later, Jaime was face to face with the Bat.

Miguel Santos was graying slightly at the temples and somewhat shorter than Jaime would have expected. Nevertheless, he exuded an air of supreme confidence.

"Welcome to Miami, Mr. Acosta. And welcome to the family. We're very pleased you could join this weekend."

Jaime managed an "honor's mine, sir," before Miguel Santos continued, sweeping his arm grandly across the room, which seemed to have grown silent with all eyes turned towards him.

"You will see CALB's importance to this community with your own eyes. You will feel it in your blood as you walk among my people. You will know, when you return to Washington, why Congress must act. We are depending on you and the great Ricardo Peralta to right the wrongs." Here, he let his gaze soften. Measuring the exact ratio of charm to gravity, Santos spoke as to a new disciple. "We will make history together, young man."

With last brief smile in Jaime's direction, Miguel Santos clapped his hands together twice and moved to take his seat at the head of the long table. His brother claimed his seat at the other end. Wordlessly, Jaime took a chair next to his boss and waited quietly for the meeting to proceed.

Tito Cortina rose and launched into a speech that Jaime had now come to recognize as standard for CALB's puppet president. He took this chance to study the faces of those around him. All were glazed expressions, dozens of dark eyes dulled with boredom, shifting only to check the sweeping hands of their gold watches. Tito went on. The sighs were audible.

"We are ready," Santos cut in, extending his hand to point at the chair he wished Tito to take: "That is enough, my brother. We will begin."

From that point on, the show belonged to Santos. Attentiveness was no longer an issue.

"Compatriots," Santos intoned, "The truth is self-evident. We know that the final battle before a blessed triumph is often fierce. It may be treacherous, but, *mis amigos*, we are close. The day of which we have dreamed for so long *es muy cerca*, very near. Vigilance is essential. Now more than ever, the people of Cuba await us. Castro will fall. We will return. This is our mission. This is our sacred honor. From the outset, villainous forces have tried to undermine us. They will not give up now. And we must not give in. The days ahead may bring sabotage and slander. Our cause will be misrepresented, we may be personally attacked, but we will not weaken. The final push is on. *La lucha al fin.* We will persevere." A pause in Santos' speech brought solemn nods and no interruptions.

"This weekend will launch our march to victory. The rally will galvanize our community. It is a call to action. We must enlist our people to duty in the crusade for those still suffering Fidel's evil dictatorship. We will tell them what to do and how to do it. They must understand that support for our friends in the U.S. Congress is more vital now than ever before. The people will hear from Representative Peralta. They will meet other honorable people of the American government who will help us explain the importance of amendments to the foreign affairs bill, and the need for a united front. We Cuban-Americans must speak with one voice. *Una voz unida.* Only then, can we drown out our enemies. It will take the commitment of hearts, minds, and pocketbooks to see this through. We shall tell them CALB holds the key to Cuba's liberation, but our community must bind together to help Congress frame our glorious return. This is the time. *Hoy!* The time for action is now!"

Standing up, with his fingers positioned on the table's edge, forming two perfectly vaulted chambers, "You are all very good to come today. We will have many opportunities to discuss tactics over the course of the weekend. I wanted to bring us all together at the start. To set the theme. And to welcome our special friend, Congressman Ricardo Peralta."

Peralta rose. *"La lucha al fin,"* his fist punched the air as a chorus of voices exploded into cheers.

MIA

Ada's heart stopped racing roughly ten minutes before the 747 touched down. It wasn't fear. She loved flying and under normal conditions, would have spent the entire flight studying the terrain through the spyglass window. Not this time, however. It wasn't just that she had run the entire length of the D terminal at Washington's Dulles Airport and still almost missed her flight. She hadn't rested for more than a few fitful hours in the last two days. She was exhausted, but nonetheless exultant. She had met her task. The overhead bin held 300 copies of "Price of Return: The Lobby to Overthrow Castro." There in black and white, a chronicle of how one organization can donate its way into the corridors of power, securing valuable allies, and grooming them to champion controversial legislative changes with far-reaching international implications. Ada could practically recite all 16-pages, including charts, from memory. The stewardess with the drink cart assumed the pretty young passenger in 12B was napping and moved on to the next isle. But behind her closed curtain of lashes, Ada was mentally reviewing her first draft of the executive summary:

...a classic case of the pay-to-play methods used by special interest groups to purchase specific policy provisions and general political favoritism. Additionally, the CALB story serves to illustrate the broader dangers of undue influence. The initiatives CALB supporters in Congress are expected to sponsor as amendments to the pending reauthorization of the Foreign Affairs Act are characterized, even by sympathetic observers, as being of

unprecedented in magnitude. The proposed amendments have two primary objectives: (1) to prohibit any foreign-owned company that conducts business with the government of Fidel Castro from importing products into the United States; and (2) to authorize payment of a billion dollars to "the new government of Cuba" immediately upon the removal of Fidel Castro as President of Cuba. Legal scholars and inter-American affairs experts quoted at length in the body of this report criticize these proposals as anti-democratic and destabilizing.

These authorities conclude that the first proposed amendment violates international law and would undoubtedly provoke strong condemnation from industrial and developing countries alike. Any such effort to blacklist "enemy traders" could cause an anti-American backlash dangerous to U.S. economic, political and strategic interests. The U.S. consumer would no doubt also suffer considerably should such a secondary embargo be imposed.

The second amendment is also highly troublesome and subject to Constitutional challenge. It commits a significant amount of American tax dollars to a government that does not currently exist. Further, it does so without any requirement that the individual or group replacing President Castro be democratically elected at the time U.S. aid funds begin to flow or at any point thereafter. In essence, the winner of a successful coup against Fidel Castro could establish a new, perhaps far more ruthless dictatorship, and still receive generous checks from Uncle Sam.

These initiatives smack of extortion and bribery unbefitting the world's greatest democracy. Must the price of liberating Cuba from Castro's control necessarily entail the sacrifice of America founding principles? Would it not be easier and cheaper for the United States to end its anachronistic policy towards Cuba by allowing American citizens to travel to Cuba and demonstrate first-hand the benefits of living in a free and open society?

Ada had initially enjoyed crafting this rhetoric. It was starting to sound over-written to her own ears though. In grad school, she'd only had to worry about the reactions of a professor. Now, she had a public audience to consider. After giving her completed draft to Peter, she'd stood by, nervously shifting from foot to foot. He read in silence. When finished, he looked up, then turned back to the first page and began editing. The red marks had stung a bit at first, yet none were gratuitous. He softened her tone in some places, sharpened it in others, resurrected her lead from burial in the fourth paragraph and at critical junctures lent coherence to the central point. A strong suspicion that 6 years in the ivory tower hadn't taught her much about media spin loomed.

Ada wished he were there on the plane beside her. Peter was taking a later flight. COG's public affairs office would be announcing the report's publication and inviting news outlets to a media briefing scheduled for 10 a.m. Saturday, a half-hour before the kick-off of the CALB rally. Peter was working the phones, giving a heads-up to contacts in the national media, as well as to some local south Florida reporters that he expected would be particularly interested in covering the story. He told Ada not to worry. He'd field questions at the press conference, if she didn't feel ready. Settle in at the hotel, he told her; we'll hook up for dinner.

There's no reason to worry, Ada reassured herself. I may be flying solo now, but I won't be when it comes to dealing with whatever response our report provokes. Turning at last to enjoy the view before landing, she got a postcard peek at a long stretch of white shore, green sea, and pink paint. Miami Beach: the million-dollar sandbar.

FAIRCHILD

Footfalls echo in the memory
Down the passage which we did not take
Towards the door we never opened

During her final semester as an undergrad, Ada confronted that timely question: "what do I want to be when I grow-up?" She made an appointment to see the campus career counselor, whose reputation as a lecher and a bore generally drove students of both sexes to steer clear of his office. But Ada wasn't the first desperate senior to buckle under to the greater pressure of limited job prospects. She put on a caftan, pinned her hair into a bun, and headed to his office.

The advisory session ended up yielding little more than funny stories to regale her friends with afterwards. The only vaguely interesting aspect of the whole ordeal resulted from the Personality & Aptitude assessment that the counselor had insisted on administering. The test's multiple-choice formula promised to match an individual's traits and abilities with an ideal occupation. The professional path prompted by Ada's responses turned out to be landscape architecture. An odd thought for a history major, perhaps. Surprising herself as much as anyone, Ada became, at least for a time, intrigued by the idea of becoming the female successor to Frederick Law Olmstead. During this brief flirtation with horticultural planning, and before deciding to apply to Stanford's graduate studies program, she'd actually done quite a lot of research on the field. Although she eventually abandoned these studies, she never lost interest. Botanical bowers became to Ada what cathedrals, art museums, and libraries are for others.

So it was that, with time to kill before Peter's arrival, Ada wasted none of it, quickly checking in at her hotel and heading right back out again. Within an hour of landing at Miami International Airport, she was in a second cab headed to Fairchild Tropical Garden.

A canopy of vibrant royal Poinciana trees – a red carpet in reverse – welcomed Ada and her driver as they turned off Old Cutler Road and passed through the gates of the largest tropical garden in the continental United States. Colonel Robert H. Montgomery, a millionaire tax accountant from New York with a passion for plants, bestowed it as gift to the city in 1938. Her guidebook promised that the 6,000 different plants within would keep even expert botanists on their toes.

Ada did her best to identify the familiar and unfamiliar among countless cycads, aroids, ferns, tropical bloomers, bromeliads, and orchids. She struggled between the pull to linger in solitary glades and the push to roam all 83 acres of lush variety. For hours, she wandered and paused, paused and wandered. Along the way, she met the occasional school group, tourist family, and grounds keeper, but for the most part, she found herself alone in paradise.

Nearing the end of her tour, she came upon one of two dramatic vistas designed by none other than Mr. Olmstead himself. The bridge-overlook afforded a commanding view of the central gardens. Ada propped herself against the trestle's coral rock railing. She held herself completely still and concentrated on tuning all her senses to capture every nuance of sight, sound, and smell. She'd done this at numerous stops along the way, collecting a series of impressions. Now, she was ready to test whether these images could be retrieved. Eyes closed, she began to recall them one by one: each of the eleven lakes, then the hibiscus garden, the rare plant house, the tropical rainforest, the palmetum, and the rock and cactus garden. Still there, she sighed. Ada had played this memory game ever since she was a child, never wanting to lose hold of a happy moment. It was, she supposed, a way of hedging bets. Past joys don't ever have to end, as long imagination can recreate them.

Eventually Ada returned from her reverie. Her wristwatch indicated that Peter's plane was due within the hour. They'd arranged to meet for dinner. She'd need to shower, dress and collect herself. She headed back to South Beach.

SO BE

Miami Beach is a man-made sandbar. Engineers cleared away
mangroves and dredged up sediment from Biscayne Bay as infill.
In the 1930s, tycoons like Alfred J. Dupont, William Randolph
Hearst, J.C. Penny and R.J. Reynolds staked their claims to prime
beach front on the northern portion of the barrier island. The
section south of Lincoln Road became known as "south beach."
Here middle-class Jews and families fleeing the Great Depression
flocked in search of warm weather. What they found was a
neighborhood betting on a novel architectural style to help reclaim
its appeal, after a devastating hurricane.

Over 800 Art Deco buildings were constructed in this decade
and the look's brand of bright modernity became ubiquitous
throughout Miami Beach proper. The undisputed locus of this
movement was South Beach's Ocean Drive, and at the heart of this
thoroughfare sat the Hotel Avalon, nestled like an aerodynamic
Necco wafer floating in warm cream. The hotel's flamboyant,
exaggerated features were a perfect example of the earlier
generation's obsession with futurism and fantasy. Her streamlined
features and exotic embellishments suffered the ravages of time
and taste, however, and for some years she lay in neglect and
disrepair. That is, until a renewed interest in "tropical deco" made
South Beach trendy again.

In 1985, when the MTV- inspired series *Miami Vice* was all
the rage, financiers rode the wave and fully restored the Avalon.
The old gal began her come back with $4 million worth of

aluminum tubing, bakelite, vitrole, glass block, and paint colored sea foam green, powder blue, and salmon pink. The rest of the neighborhood followed suit.

Though tourism along Ocean Drive was now booming, rates remained affordable. South Beach didn't have the capacity to attract convention bookings. So, for a non-profit organization, it was an achievable choice. Peter figured booking rooms at the Avalon would please COG's accountant and make for a more appealing stay than some Marriott downtown.

It was in the Hotel Avalon's lobby that Ada and Peter had arranged to meet. As a clock festooned with feathers and shaped like a flamingo struck the appointed hour, Peter stood waiting near the bellhop's desk. He looked out across the road and beyond the flat sandy beach to the ocean. The sun was beginning to set, bathing the scene in honey.

He hadn't noticed Ada approach. It was only when he turned slightly to follow a bird in flight that he recognized her. She was looking, as he had been, at the water. Washington D.C. muted all that wasn't marble and granite. South Florida seemed to have the opposite effect; it suffused everything with light. Ada was no exception. She glowed. Her golden hair shimmered. Her grayish eyes picked up the color of the deepening indigo sky and her pale skin shone. Peter watched, aware that the sun would soon dip into the ocean and break the spell.

He saw her smile bloom, as the sun took its final bow. Then she turned to him and waved.

"Beautiful, wasn't it?"

"Absolutely," Peter replied.

"Good flight?"

"Fine. I see you made it okay, too. All settled? No problems?"

"None, everything's great. I love the hotel and the weather's superb." Ada hoped to appear professional, unflustered. She'd even made a point of dressing conservatively, even though the resort atmosphere (not to mention the surfeit of fashion models in micro-minis) made her want to slip into something more sparce. Writing the report had kept her too busy over the last couple days to worry about any incipient feelings for Peter. Once in Miami, however, it dawned on her they'd be together the whole weekend, side by side.

She didn't want to embarrass herself or him with a silly schoolgirl crush. There was no need to bare her long legs. Tonight, slacks.

They chatted a bit more before Ada confided: "I was so nervous that I wouldn't even let the airline people take my luggage. I insisted on lugging the box of reports on the plane with me to keep in the overhead. I didn't want them ending up in Milwaukee by mistake."

They laughed. "But you're relaxed now, aren't you?"

"Fully recovered, I'm happy to report. Ready to enter the fray."

"I know you are," he said to reassure her.

"So, what have I missed since this morning?" she asked.

"The report's already kicking up a stir. I fielded more calls than I placed today. I expect we'll get a big turn-out for the press conference. *NPR* and *CNN* are both sending a crew. *Newsweek's* interested. A freelancer I know from *Harper's Monthly* may also show up."

"Really? There's that much interest in a report?"

"A couple of things are working in our favor. We're piggybacking on the coverage of CALB's bigger event. Our bit adds a different angle that'll help round out a story on the overall issue for the reporters who had already planned to be here. Another plus is that our report is essentially an exposé, which makes it an easy way for a journalist to look hard-hitting. And finally, the public is cynical; people are sick of politics as usual, so any news piece that confirms their worst suspicions about official corruption gets audience."

Ada nodded. "Well," she offered, "then it's a good thing we chose an open space for the press conference."

"There's one more thing I haven't mentioned, but why don't I fill you in over dinner." Peter began walking down the stairs to the street "we'll just roam until we find a good spot."

The pair ambled along, surrounded by sunburned visitors and bronzed locals. They rejected a few spots before entering the portico of *Bistro Plato*.

THE CAVE

"Drink?" Peter suggested, once they'd settled into one of the quieter tables on the outside terrace. The decor, just a touch overdone, was nonetheless appealing. A pleasant grotto-like atmosphere had been achieved with the aid of vine-draped archways, shadow-casting torches, gurgling stone fountains, soft Mediterranean music, and frescoed walls depicting figures dancing on a cave wall.

"How does one get service in this republic?

Just then, a man with what looked to be a facsimile of a stone tablet arrived. "Would you care to see the wine list, sir?"

"Thank you," Peter accepted the proffered object. "Any preferences I should know about, Ada?"

"Would you mind red?"

Peter handed the tablet back. "Margaux. The Segla. And some menus please."

"Right away, sir. "

When they were alone again, Ada pressed. "What's the rest of your news?"

"The Honorable Benjamin O. Davey."

"Is?"

"A five term Democrat from West Roxbury, Massachusetts. First black man ever elected to Congress from that State."

"Is he the one who jokes that a clever logo designer got him elected? The fillagree over his middle initial making his campaign posters look like a call to vote for candidate O'Davey?"

"The very one."

"What about him?"

"He's coming."

"To Miami?"

"To the press conference."

"Really?"

"Benny O. Davey's been active on Cuba issues for years. His presence will bolster our message. I can speak to the issue of undue influence and the damage CALB's tactics wreck upon our institutions and processes. Ben has the authority to cover the foreign relations angle; the harm done to American interests abroad and to the Cuban people who are caught in the middle of an old Cold War fight, etc. He can remind the press that a sizable percentage of the island population is black. It's actually these and other ordinary Cuban citizens, who bear the brunt of the U.S. embargo. He can explain that the ban on trade in food and medicine impacts hunger and illness, and that it actually enables Castro to heap all the blame for dire conditions on cruel *Yanqui* imperialists."

Ada gestured for him to continue.

"Congressman Davey was a pediatrician before being elected to the House. Last year, he joined a group of doctors and health inspectors that visited Cuba as part of a United Nations fact-finding mission. He's seen the suffering our policies have caused and wants to reform them on both humanitarian and policy grounds. He makes a powerful argument. It'll be great to have him up on stage."

"Amazing. How did you get him to do it?"

"Actually, he invited himself. He'd read an advance copy of the report last night and called this morning, asking to participate."

"An advance copy?"

"Ada," Peter joked, "are you preparing me for tomorrow's grilling by the press?"

"Frank Wayne gave it to him." She was learning fast. An almost imperceptible look of delight crept into the corners of her smile.

"Surprised?" he asked.

"Not really."

"Didn't think so." They both began to laugh. Peter leaned forward with a grin. "So?"

"It's brilliant. How do they know each other?"

"Old friends and former associates from Frank's days in government."

This time, Ada was surprised. She bent slightly towards him as though to hear better, "Did I miss something between Frank's many tall tales? Like a career in government that he failed to mention?"

Peter filled in the gaps. He explained that Frank seldom speaks of his stint in the service of Uncle Sam. Ada listened intently as Peter recounted the story of young Frank Wayne's promising rise through the ranks of the diplomatic corps, the brutal circumstances of his disillusionment, and his abrupt resignation. Let down by his country and betrayed by the woman he loved, had prompted Frank to wander for years through distant lands, never returning to the island at the center of his grief.

Perhaps it was the fact that she herself knew Frank or maybe it was simply hearing the strained emotion in Peter's voice as he spoke, but when his story had ended Ada believed no Greek playwright or Elizabethan bard had ever made her feel so sad. She could only shake her head.

The silence was broken by the arrival of their meal. After the waiter withdrew. Peter reached across and momentarily covered her hand with his.

She allowed herself a quick pause, then transferred her attention to the plate before her. "We shouldn't let it get cold" adding, "I'm okay, Peter, just sentimental by nature." As if to prove her resolve, she clutched her fork.

Peter tasted his selection and made approving sounds.

Ada seemed just to be moving her risotto around.

"I'm sorry, Ada, I didn't mean to steal your appetite. Frank's fine now. You've seen him. He's made peace with the past."

"Of course. But are you sure it's wise to get him involved in our project? Won't it stir up memories?"

"That's a legitimate concern. It's just that when you came along..."

"Me?"

"I'll try to explain. Do you remember that first weekend we met at the office and you started asking me all about Santos?" Ada nodded for him to continue, "As you've pointed out, I could have told you all you needed to know then and there. But a recollection struck me. Years ago, I'd asked Frank pretty much the same thing, you know, about Santos and the exiles. Frank just came alive talking about it all. It was like he started to see a way to come to terms with events in his past. He recognized an opportunity to exact, not revenge, but some degree of resolution simply by talking. I think it was healthy to have him talk about Cuba again."

Not wanting to interfere with the flow, Ada nodded.

"Unfortunately, my investigations at that point didn't amount to much, and at that early stage in my career I wasn't really in a position to affect change anyway. I let it go, but I felt I'd let him down." Peter drew a breath, "Ada, I knew for sure when you started pulling at these strings that this time it would be different. I could tell you were onto something we could really use. When I sent you to Frank, it was for his illumination as much as yours. I thought that seeing you – young, beautiful, curious – would bring back Frank's fighting spirit...and it has. I've never seen him more energized. Since I've known him, he's shied away from people who reminded him of bygone days; but now, all of a sudden, he's fired up to call old cronies like Ben O. Davey and hop back into the fray."

"Leaking the report to Davey was Frank's idea?"

"Yes."

Ada took a minute to select from the many questions she wanted to ask. She decided to start at square one: "Peter, how do you even know Frank?"

"He's my godfather."

"Oh."

"My parents were foreign service officers. They sent me to a boarding school when I was young. This was a long time ago" he declared reflectively. "I used to write to them care of the State Department because their postings were always a secret. They were Sovietologists. I just assumed they were living somewhere behind the Iron Curtain." Ada watched his frown deepen. He spoke hurriedly, "They died a month before my high-school graduation. No idea where or how or why. Frank came to see me and broke the bad news. I'd only met him once before. He took an apartment in town and hung out until my classes were over. Then he helped me pack up and brought me back to Georgetown with him. I lived with him until going off to college and came back to him on breaks. He's my only family. And I'm his. Two lost sailors."

Ada's expression was blank. "Hey," Peter called. She looked at him, her grey eyes clouding with tears.

"I can't even imagine." She gave a kind of nervous laugh, "boy, these working dinners can be intense."

Peter shifted his chair alongside hers. "I didn't mean to make you sad. I thought telling you might...."

"Oh, don't worry about me," she hesitated, "it sounds like you're talking about all this for the first time."

"I am."

She turned to him, "Let's go to the ocean."

"Lead the way." Peter left money for the bill, grabbed the bottle by the neck, and offered her his arm.

THE SANDS

By 6:30 a.m., Ada was back from a salty sprint along the sand. She'd spent her early morning run reflecting upon the previous evening and the long day ahead. She and Peter had mostly listened to the sound of the water, as they sat at the edge of the shore after dinner. When they parted back at the hotel, they made plans to meet for breakfast.

Ada calculated that she still had an hour or so to get ready for their morning rendezvous. Plenty of time to stretch out and observe South Beach rise lazily to meet the day. Bent over with her nose to her knee, she saw another runner approach. Even viewed laterally and with the distortion of speed, she recognized Peter's long-limbed gait. Soon enough, he was there on the grassy verge beside her.

"Hi," he panted.

"Morning," Ada called back brightly. "We should have coordinated," adding, "that is, if you like company."

"Of course. Tomorrow. A run before our flight."

"Great. If I make it through today. Speaking of which," she brushed the sweat from her forehead, "I'd better clean up and get organized. Meet you back here at 7:30," she confirmed.

"Yep."

Ada stretched to full height, brushing sand from her legs as she crossed Ocean Avenue and reentered the hotel.

CAMP FIRE

The evening of his arrival, Jaime dined with fellow Hill staffers whose bosses were also attending the Miami rally at Miguel Santos' invitation. CALB had booked a private room at a trendy restaurant convenient to the Congressional delegation's hotel. There, the legislative assistants entertained themselves, while their Members were busy flashing teeth, gushing interest, and pocketing checks at a lavish fundraiser.

The price of a free meal in Washington usually entailed making a certain amount of polite conversation with one's hosts. It was a rare treat indeed when a House or Senate aide could mingle solely with his or her own kind at a work-related event. Here they were now, with an open tab and nary a lobbyist or supervising adult in sight. Appreciating these special circumstances, they raised many a margarita to toast their absent benefactors. The tributes grew louder and more raucous, until, full of drink and delicacies, Jaime and his colleagues stumbled back to the Fountain Bleu and crawled into their, for the most part, respective beds. Alone in his, Jaime was rudely awakened at the crack of dawn by a pounding headache made worse by the steady recurrence of a shrill, nagging ring. Dazed and not amused, he finally acknowledged the call.

"Hello," he grumbled into the phone.

"Jaime? It's Oscar."

"God damn, Oscar. What time is it?"

"Sorry to wake you, but my boss just hauled my sorry ass out of bed and put me in charge of rounding up the group. Apparently, the guys at CALB got wind of a protest event. Tito Cortina's all freaked out. He's already on his way to the hotel to brief us."

"Shit. So early in the morning?"

"I hear you, dude. No choice. Half an hour, in the Sonesta Lounge. Meet you there."

Jaime hung up the phone. Tequila, *te sufre,* he thought to himself.

SHADOW BOX

Mrs. Santos sat in silence. White knuckles betrayed her. Her bloodless fingers bore into the book she'd been reading. She shook with the approach of the man to whom she was married.

He thundered in, shaking his fist and sputtering with unsuppressed rage. In this state, Miguel Santos presented a much different portrait than his adoring supporters were accustomed to seeing. His wife seldom saw anything else. She'd witnessed his manic fury many times. He would bellow and rail against external tormentors, then turn his attention to her. Some effort might have succeeded in defusing him, but she never uttered a word, nor did she break her concentrated look of loathing, even after blows began to fall.

"*Cuando*, Carolina? When will they stop persecuting me for my convictions? How many more betrayals must our people endure? *Porque*? We are so close. So close!" His bulging eyes glared at her. "It never ends! Dupes at the *New York Times* make Fidel a hero, as our island is sold to the Soviets. Then, Kennedy breaks his promise and abandons our fighters to die like slaughtered pigs on the beaches. And now the agents of evil rise again. I will not be defeated. I will NOT! Do you hear me, Carolina? You listen well, my wife! Lying words and false reports will not bring me down. Nothing can stop what I alone have set in motion!" He stood directly before her now, his fist upraised. "Have you nothing to say, Carolina?" he demanded.

She merely turned her head to the side and promised herself she would not flinch.

"Very well," he sputtered, preparing to strike. A loud knock at the door interrupted him. With his arm still suspended, Santos considered his next move. Gratifying as it would have been to wipe that look of disgust from his wife's face, he was anxious for news.

As consolation, he snatched the book from her hands and tore it in half. With a final flourish, he hurled the pieces against the wall, spat at her feet, and stormed out to receive his visitor.

Left alone, Carolina began to shake. She would not cry. Composing herself, she stole soundlessly across the passage to the bathroom adjacent to her husband's study. It was from this listening post, with her ear pressed to the wall, that she had succeeded in discovering his secrets many times before.

On this occasion, she heard the voice of her imbecile brother-in-law, Tito Cortina. He was endeavoring to assure Santos that everything was under control. Santos did not sound convinced.

"You have, as always, missed the point, dear brother. It is not I who fears the press, Tito; it is these preening politicians. They bend over and cup their *cojones* when the media press them. I see that I must handle it myself. I will call the Congressmen and make things crystal clear. They must know that loyalty carries a high price. We will deliver only if they support us. If they try to distance themselves, the money will dry up. Or, far worse." Adding ominously, "Our community has its radicals, Tito. I would hate to see those who practice their war games in the Everglades come out and target any of our good friends. I have no control over these stealth fighters. It would be most unfortunate..." his voice trailed off, as though the thought was too unpleasant to pursue – or too delicious to share.

Tito spoke again at this point, but Carolina couldn't catch more than the occasional word. A maid had begun vacuuming the rooms overhead. When the noise stopped and she could eavesdrop again, she heard Santos speaking to a silent third party. He's on the phone, she surmised. His tone was stern but diplomatic. Maybe it's one of his politicians, she thought. Quietly, Mrs. Santos exited the bathroom and made her way upstairs. He will leave soon. Then I can think.

Chapter 5

MONDAY 1996

CNN ran with amateur video footage shot by an attendee. An *Associated Press* stringer put the news out over the wires within minutes. But the *South Florida Sentinel* was the first to get the story into print, with three hastily scribed paragraphs in its Saturday afternoon edition:

Dueling Demonstrations on Cuba Policy Turn Bloody
Violence erupted today in Miami's Little Havana neighborhood, as hundreds of people participating in a rally sponsored by the powerful exile organization, the Cuban American Liberation Bond, clashed with individuals attending a nearby press conference. Dozens of bystanders were injured, some seriously, as angry demonstrators disrupted a meeting at Independence Park, organized by Citizens for Open Government, a Washington, D.C.- based political research foundation. The watchdog group, well known for its vocal advocacy of campaign finance reform, called the press conference to announce the release of a new report criticizing the Cuban American Liberation Bond's (CALB) lobbying efforts. Shortly before the disturbance began, prominent spokesperson for the exile group, Mr. Miguel Santos, President of Santos Fiesta Cruise Lines, denounced the report as "treasonous" and called upon the crowd to "repel, defeat, destroy enemies of freedom." According to witnesses, the gathered masses began marching towards the site of the Citizens for Open Government event, waving placards and later using them to strike at attendees.

The Citizens for Open Government report contends that Mr. Santos and other CALB representatives exercise undue influence over the United States policy towards the government of Cuban President Fidel Castro, as a result of the access to certain policymakers that generous campaign contributions have afforded. According to the Federal Election Commission, through its political action committee and its members, CALB has given over $550,000 to U.S. elected officials from both political parties since 1994. Several Members of Congress, each of whom receive significant financial support from the hardline anti-Castro organization, participated in the rally. New Jersey Congressman Richard Peralta defended his role at the CALB event as "thoroughly appropriate." Referring to the bloody skirmish initiated by CALB backers, Representative Peralta added: "It was an unfortunate incident. But the public should not be misled. The altercation was provoked. The crowd was only trying to defend against those who seek to subvert the victory of the Cuban people over the tyranny of Fidel Castro."

Congressman Ben O. Davey of Massachusetts, present to endorse the Citizens for Open Government report, offered a much different perspective than his colleague. "Silencing those who disagree through violent means is not the way to foster peaceful, democratic change in Cuba or anywhere else. Giving lip service to free speech is not enough. Leaders must practice what they preach."

BLUE NOTE

The man in the red baseball cap closed his notebook, clicked his pen, and placed both in the back pocket of his faded blue jeans. Peter pressed a business card into his palm, "Good luck," he said. The reporter smirked, "I'm off to find a 'startled bystander.' Can't file without the full formula. Editors…" he muttered, wandering off.

Peter took a deep breath and stretched. He raised his arms over his head and let out a slow whistle. Peter had long since removed his suit coat, but it hadn't made much difference. Sweat rolled down his neck. The shirt plastered to his back made his skin feel shrink-wrapped. He imagined diving into the ocean and letting the salt water suspend the need to do anything other than float.

Time to regroup, he thought. He ran a hand through his hair and sighed, setting off to find Ben.

Peter found him smoking a pipe in the selective shade of a Royal Palm tree.

"Quite a day" Peter proclaimed, "you don't look the worse for wear."

"More than I can say for you."

"Been working, man. Got to feed the fish when they're in a frenzy."

"Oh, I know. You've been doing such a fine job. I've kept an eye out," Ben winked.

"Uh-huh. And I've been watching you hold court under this tree, letting the piranhas come to you. Don't think I fail to recognize the greater wisdom of your approach, but I still have to shop my spin around. Know what I mean?"

"Indeed, I do. And more power to you, brother," the older man gave him a loose salute.

They stood together surveying the scene – departing newsies, a couple of cops on horses, random gawkers, and few vagrants wondering when they'd get their park back.

"How about the young lady? She looks a bit shaken," Ben asked inclining his head towards the eastern edge of the stage.

Peter tracked Ben's nod and spotted Ada leaning against a local television news truck. "I'll go check. I think we're about done here anyhow," he said. Still watching her, Peter added, "Why don't you take off."

"Yes."

Peter smiled, "you're a good man, Benny." They shook hands, "Buy you a drink back at your hotel? Hour or so."

"I'll expect to see you both in one hour," the honorary Irishman commanded. Oh, and Peter," he added, placing a hand on the taller man's arm, "I'll be giving Frank a call. He'll want to know what's happened."

"Of course, thanks."

Peter was waylaid by a metro policeman, but eventually, made it over to his research assistant's side. Ada's equilibrium was slowly returning. The melee had been frightening. She never witnessed a physical altercation before, much less been a motivating factor in one. Having to deal with the press had helped her act somewhat normal in the moments immediately following the crisis. But then, after most of the reporters had hustled off to file their pieces, she was left hanging. So, she hung, staring off into space. That's where she was when Peter found her.

"Wild launch party," he said lightly. A faint smile flickered across her lips. "Are you okay?" he asked.

When she hadn't responded for some seconds, he bent down to her eye level. Gingerly, he nudged her chin until she faced him.

"It's curious," she said vaguely, "Why isn't 'daymare' a word?"

"Day-what?"

"You know," turning towards him, "Like a nightmare but when you're awake."

Peter laid a hand on her shoulder "A 'mare's a 'mare."

"Is that Mr. Ed or Gertrude Stein?"

"Come on," he coaxed her away from the truck, "let's get out of here."

They walked like that, his arm over her shoulder and hers about his waist, past the torch of Independence that gave the park its name. Peter didn't release his grip until they reached the rental car. He unlocked the door and held it open for her. With Ada seated on the passenger side, he knelt down to see if the distant stare remained. It was gone.

Ada pulled him roughly across her on the car seat; he pressed down, covering her mouth with his. The embrace ended as suddenly as it began. Peter rocked back on his heels and stood up. He went around to the driver's side and got in. They were both still breathing heavily. He turned on the ignition and peeled out of the lot.

Neither said a word until they passed the toll both on the Venetian Bridge. Peter steered the car to the side of the road and let the engine idle. He turned toward her, "I don't know what came over me, Ada. I'm sorry."

"No, no, it was my fault," her voice cracked. "It was just, you know, this afternoon was so crazy. I think I'm in shock or something."

"No, I…" hesitating, "it won't happen again."

"Deal."

"Deal."

Peter steered back onto the road. "I told Ben we'd have a drink with him. We should probably head over there soon. If that's all right?"

"I'd like that."

"Cool. He's up the road a couple blocks."

They found the Hotel Del Mar easily enough. As they were mounting the coral rock steps to the reception area, Ada grabbed Peter's sleeve. He could see she was weighing her words.

"Peter. It's really no biggie. I mean, everything copacetic, right? You know, for us to work together."

Peter aimed a brotherly cuff at her arm. "Yes. It'll all be fine."

SLIDING DOORS

Peter and Ada were ordering a second round when the Honorable Ben O. Davey joined them in his hotel's oceanside lounge. He added a scotch to the tab and apologized for keeping them. Ada decided that, dressed in jeans, a faded oxford, and topsiders, the legendary civil rights leader looked less imposing. Or maybe it had something to do with the bonding effect of shared calamity. Possibly it was simply Ben's unassuming way that had transformed her awe to affectionate respect. She was happy to see him, and, truth-be-told, relieved to have a third person there to help keep her mind off of Peter.

After gaining reassurance from Ada that she'd fully recovered from the afternoon's excitement, Ben explained his tardiness: "I've been having the most interesting phone conversation with Brooke Glaze from *The Washington Post*. She'd left a message at the front desk for me to call as soon as got in. Well, I thought to myself, what's so urgent? Could she be working on a story about today's little scuffle? No, that can't be it, I reasoned, Brooke's an investigative reporter, not a correspondent. It must be something else. So, giving in to curiosity, I gave her a bell. She pussyfooted around at first – how've I been, what's the hot committee gossip, blah blah blah – but then, she started asking me what I could tell her about the Cabal's antics, past and present. She asked about my interest in promoting the COG report. When did I first meet Miguel Santos, and such."

"Where's this coming from?" Peter wondered.

"That's the most intriguing part." Ben continued, "I've known Brooke Glaze for many years. I've given her dozens of interviews on and off the record. I know the difference between Brooke's fishing with an empty hook and Brooke dangling a juicy hunk of bait. Let me tell you, I could smell a squirming worm right through the receiver. She's gotten a hold of something. That's for sure. I don't know who's feeding her tips. Or why. Or even what it is she's hoping to catch. But she's already doing some pretty heavy casting by calling me up out of the blue." Ben seemed to slip away with his own thoughts.

"What did you tell her?"

"Enough to whet the appetite. I suggested that I might have plenty of colorful anecdotes and budding scandals to trade with her. Contingent, of course, upon her sharing a bit with me."

"Do you think she'll tell you what she's heard?" Ada asked.

"To a certain extent; it'll be unavoidable. The more specific her questions become, the better I'll know what she's after. Brooke's very savvy, she'll look around, try to get her info for free first. But then she'll realize she can't and come back ready to give in order to get. I told her to call my office on Monday. I'm hoping we'll start the bidding then."

Ada began to say something, but the pressure of Peter's leg against hers made her stop. Startled, and not a little embarrassed, she shot him an anxious look. His expression halted her pique, and she followed the tilt of his head indicating the arrival of a large group, which was rapidly filling in the tables in their section of the lounge. Ada registered that they were now in earshot of others, but when neither Peter nor Ben spoke again, she took a more careful look and found her gaze lock on the shining black eyes of the man himself, *el Murcielago*. No longer shouting in impassioned anger, as he had been earlier on the ceiling-mounted television monitor at the bar, he was now holding court with obsequious smiles. Ada too received his treatment. Upon catching her eye, he gave her a once-over that make her feel dirty and ashamed.

Ada shifted away from Santos' scrutiny. She focused first on the nautical decorations lining the back wall of the lounge, then stole another glance at what she supposed must be a gathering of the Cabal and its supporters. It was among that crowd that she found a different set of eyes bearing down on her. Jaime's. It shouldn't have been such a shock. She'd blocked from her thoughts the possibility of seeing him. It had all been so crazy – the rushed decision to issue the report, flying to Miami, planning the press thing, dealing with rioting invaders, then Peter and… but hell, still, she ought to have considered this. She had known he'd be there. He'd told her himself about the trip. She'd wished him bon voyage. And here she was now sitting with people that she imagined he must consider enemies. What's that phrase: the enemy of my friend is my enemy...something like that.

Peter and Ben were rising to leave. There was nothing she could do but follow. She had to pass by Jaime's chair on the way out. The two classmates exchanged mirror images of hurt and confusion.

TOUCHING GREY

The lobby of the Hotel Del Mar was virtually empty when Ada caught up moments later with Ben and Peter, who were talking by a marble fountain with a statue of Ponce De Leon rising in triumph from its center.

As she approached, Ben was saying: "looks like the Good Old Grey's been beaten to the punch."

"Maybe the Post wasn't the only paper that the tipster contacted," Peter ventured, "the more the merrier. Let's just hope whoever writes it scores a hit."

Ben bowed to them both and took his leave.

The sun had softened, and a gentle breeze stirred the hotel's well-tended gardenia bushes, scenting the air with sweet fragrance. The setting intensified Ada's melancholic mood.

They stood quietly looking into the fountain.

"My friend is here. He's part of Santos' party."

Peter listened as Ada told him about seeing Jaime moments before and about their earlier lunch at the Hawk & Dove. She confessed to feeling low and false like she'd been caught cheating. They'd begun walking and by the time she finished, they had arrived back at the Avalon. Peter didn't say anything, figuring he could walk back for the rental car tomorrow.

"Let's sit," he said steering her towards the sea wall across from their hotel. "Ada, you didn't do anything wrong. Your friend has a job. You have a job. Washington is a town defined by differing opinions and competing agendas. Some friendships survive political differences, and some don't."

He could see her tense up and broke off, chastened by his own cynicism. "It's not that I believe friendship is expendable. In fact, I think just the opposite. Friends, true friends, need to respect that sometimes they'll disagree. Our democracy would be better off if we focus on what unites us rather than divides." He took her hand. "You and Jaime can sort this out. Okay, so you didn't clue him in on your research, but you hadn't fully made the connection with his boss in a way that registered to you. That wasn't deceitful. You established a sensible buffer zone. Think about it. If you had rung Jaime up once you knew we'd be publishing the report and you'd be coming down here, what would he have done? Would he have kept it to himself, hence betraying his boss? Or would he have tipped off Peralta and Santos, hence betraying you?"

"I see what you're saying, but it still feels...I dunno..."

"Messy. Life has plenty of grey areas and it's a good thing to recognize them when they appear. The people that worry me the most are the ones who insist on drawing lines in black and white, defining what's good and bad. That's the trouble with Santos," Peter paused, "it's all or nothing with him. He's extreme, myopic; he can't recognize the inconsistencies rampant throughout his platform. He rants and raves about democracy; yet stifles any competing opinions. He spouts off about his people being oppressed, but then pushes embargo policies that keep them hungry and sick. He says he's for open markets, free elections, but he's already got a new Cuban constitution written and a dozen monopoly business deals locked up. He's all hubris and hypocrisy. You don't want to think like that, Ada. Don't let any of this stuff get in the way of the people you care about. Policy disputes will always be there, close friends will not."

"But Jaime admires Santos."

"Just let it be understood that on this issue you and he will have to agree to disagree. Sit down with him next week and have a good talk, you'll straighten all this out."

"I hope so."

Peter hopped up on the wall beside her. "Look, I'll tell you something I probably shouldn't. Until now, I've always worked

Alone. That's how I wanted it. I'm not sure what possessed me to offer you a role on this project…"

She looked down, fearing the worst.

"Hey, let me finish. What I mean is that I'm glad I gave in to whatever the hell it was that made me ask for your help." That got a smile. "It's like I explained about bringing Frank in on this, getting him back in the saddle again – you were the reason behind that. You're having a positive effect on me too. Don't underestimate what you're capable of with your good instincts. Trust yourself. That's all I'm saying."

"Now I don't know what to say."

"Why say anything? Come on, it's been a long, hard day." Peter stood up, "you must be exhausted."

"Actually, I feel wired. I'm not ready to turn in."

"How about a game of pool? Clear sides, easy rules."

"I'm in! Is there a table around here?

"I seem to recall a place near where we parked. We should retrieve the car anyway. The Deuce Club, I think. We'll play a bit, grab a bite, and then call it a night."

"Back to the old grind tomorrow."

"Already old, huh?"

Ada smiled, a big wide grin, the first in some hours.

Chapter 6

A TUESDAY 1996

"Glaze."

"Do you recognize my voice?"

"Yes. I'm glad you called back. You were right. There was an incident in Miami, as you said. I guess that's not news to you."

"No."

"Can you tell me how you came to know in advance?"

"I cannot."

"Why give me the heads up then?"

"I need you to believe me. I wanted to show you that I know many things, secret things. I can tell them to you, but you need to take me seriously, to trust that I speak the truth. This allowed me to demonstrate that my information is accurate."

"You passed your test."

"Yes."

"Okay. I'm all ears."

"Good. Have you become curious about the principal? He who incited the demonstrators to attack."

"Miguel Santos is a very public figure with a very public history already."

"In the comic books, certain characters wear eye-catching costumes to disguise their identities. Why should real life be any different?"

"Do you know what's behind the mask then?"

"Keep digging, Miss Glaze. I will call you again in one week."

BEDROCK

True to form, Monday dragged. Ada remained wholly uninspired from start to quit. Peter had been out of the office in meetings all day. She spent the long intervening hours sending faxes and taking calls. COG's press office had been inundated with requests for the "Bat Brief," as coined by a local NBC affiliate.
Journalists from all over the world wanted copies of the report behind the riot. A British tabloid, boastful of being the Kingdom's kinkiest, was particularly interested to gain photographic proof of rumors that *El Murcielago* wore black leather.

By day's end, Ada was beat. Spent, but antsy. She was too full of fidget to go straight home. What to do? Maybe a girl's night out. That's the ticket. She dialed up Lindy and Kermit.

An hour later the three young women were swelling pockets around the green felt tables of Bedrock Billiards. Racking up round after round, shattering male concentration levels with each sinking shot. The girls were having a ball. The pool parlor's quirky aura was ideal for those looking to leave the daily grind behind. It had kind of an *après* ski-cum-hunting lodge decor. The mounted heads of imaginary forest dwellers shared wall space with jazz age prints and dated sports gear. Resting comfortably on well-worn kilim rugs were rustic couches from some designer's Sundance collection and tables carved to resemble creatures from a Hieronymus Bosch painting. A CD jukebox revolved an eclectic blend of hits – from Sinatra to Tom Waits, Jane's Addiction to the Barenaked Ladies.

Ada, on this particular evening, was proving master of the felt. The game was cutthroat; Ada had chosen high balls, Lindy the low and Kermit got stuck with the fast-falling middle. It was Ada's turn. She pressed her attack.

"Stop sharking, Ada! Why don't you go after someone else's for a change?" Kermit cried in good-humored frustration.

"Nothing personal, kiddo. Your guys just had a rough break," Ada observed, as she deep-sixed the 8-ball, "they landed in all the wrong spots." She sized up the remaining field and re-chalked by holding the stick against her hand and deftly shifting of her foot back and forth to make it rotate, "if it makes you feel better, Lindy's 3-ball is about to drop down the left corner rabbit hole." And so it went, through the looking glass.

"Lindy," Kermit inquired, "does Ada's sudden acquisition of stellar pool technique not make you suspicious? Seems like maybe there's more to this story than meets the eye," she added cocking an eyebrow for fullest effect.

"Yes. My theory is that she lost her job and has been spending her days in pool halls, putting the sting on unsuspecting lobbyists too busy watching her stretch for the long shots to realize that she was bleeding them dry."

"Busted." Ada crossed her wrists, "Cuff me."

"Will you confess?"

"Let's sit down so we can all catch up!"

Kermit went first and wasted little time revealing the details of a series of unproductive dalliances, mostly with young men she'd met through work. As she told it, with these guys, she'd engage in fascinating conversations about timber policy, travels in Tibet, and Boulder's best brew pubs, but the spark of mutual physical attraction never seemed to flicker.

This wasn't nearly as steamy as the tales Lindy had to tell. She had been dating the executive producer of a well-known Sunday talk show. He was twenty years older than she, but a hunk, according to Kermit who'd met him. Things seemed to be getting pretty serious. A romantic trip to St. Lucia was already in the works for next month.

"So," Ada led casually, "I guess...you all don't see anything wrong with becoming involved with someone from work then?"

"I don't see anything wrong with it," Kermit looked at Lindy.

"Doable. Not optimal. But, once you're out of school, how else are you going to meet new people? It just happens that way," Lindy shrugged. "Why not? At least you know you have one thing in common."

Ada squinted, thinking. Her two friends exchanged glances.

"That wasn't a hypothetical question was it? Who's the colleague?"

"And how far has it gone?" Lindy pressed.

"Nowhere. No one." Ada wavered, "Nothing yet, anyhow." Her friends weren't buying it. "It's just a crush thing. Stupid, really, as he's my boss and all."

"Your boss!" Kermit gasped, "Oh, Ada, spill."

"There's no hanky-panky," Ada shifted uncomfortably, "I'm just spending entirely too much time thinking about him." She took a breath, "We were down in Miami together..."

Ada filled the girls in on the fateful weekend in the tropics, including the fact that Jaime had been there too, in an opposing capacity. Simply giving voice to all the pent-up emotions inside of her was a tremendous release. Ada headed home that night more relaxed and lucid.

She was feeling good as she reached the entry to her apartment building. She opened the front door, as an unwelcome thought intervened. What if that was it? The report was done. Project over. Did that mean it was back to the intern pit? What a crushing disappointment that would be.

Ada entered her flat, flipped on the stereo, flopped down on the bed, and let Bob Dylan take over.

Forgot about that simple twist of fate.

TIGHT ROLL

"We do campaign finance, not foreign affairs," Peter was saying, "Not that I wouldn't love to jump in and stir the pot."

"You already have, it seems to me," Frank interjected.

"Yes, but that was an outcome, not an objective."

"Oh," his shrewd blue eyes twinkling, "I see. The splitting of hairs."

"Is that a question or a comment?"

"My boy, I do miss spending time with you. It does me a world of good."

Peter relaxed and lit the cigar Frank had offered him. Peter wasn't much of a smoker. He only did so to keep Frank company. He could see Frank studying him closely through the flare of the match.

Peter ventured back in gingerly. "Seriously, this is outside of COG's bailiwick. I can't play lone crusader. I have to abide by our guiding principles. We've issued our report...now it's up to the human rights groups and members of Congress like Ben to fight the legislation. We illuminate. They agitate. It's their fight now, not COG's."

"You don't believe it's your fight?"

Peter sighed. "This isn't personal, Frank. I have to remember what my job is. COG's mission is transparency and accountability in elections. We shine a light on malfeasance and make recommendations, but we don't lobby. Our non-profit tax status won't allow it."

"Can you just walk away? You don't even want to try influencing the course of proceedings, preventing bad legislation from becoming law?"

"Frank, there are many things I hope to do in this life. My current occupation keeps me focused on one for now. I'm not able to run off on a...now don't look at me like that."

"What?"

"Like you're disappointed. Damn it, Frank." Peter drew in a long breath and seemed to come to a decision. "Okay, here's the limit. I will strategize behind the scenes with you, but nothing official. I'm a concerned *private* citizen acting *outside* of COG's mantle. I can't involve the organization."

"Tremendous, Peter." Frank clasped his hand, "I'm ever so pleased. I know Ada will be too."

"Ada?" Peter pulled back, "I just told you, this is strictly a clandestine undertaking."

"Oh, but surely, you didn't mean to exclude her. In fact, you'll need a new reason for her to hang around your office now. If you want to keep her" correcting himself, "that is, I mean, if you want to keep mentoring her."

"Okay, that's enough." Peter held up his hand, "I need to think this through."

"Your best interests and our success are my only motives, Peter. Why don't we speak again tomorrow? In fact, why don't you join Ben and me for breakfast?"

"Ben?"

"Yes. Old Ebbit Grill. 8 a.m." Frank tried in vain to suppress a smile, "We have made a reservation for four."

"Why do I even bother?" Peter shook his head laughing, "Fine, we'll both be there."

DIAS BIAS

Reporters clustered around the designated media table at the left side of the hearing room, talking amongst themselves or picking away at the stale remains of a pastry tray.

Jaime grunted cynically and redirected his gaze to the faces in the main gallery. Mentally, he divided those seated in the public area into three categories: lobbyists; staffers; and tourists. The audience, unlike the press scrum, seemed attentive to the Chairman's opening remarks. On this count alone, Jaime was aligned with the muckrakers. He'd learned quickly to turn a deaf ear to the distinguished gentleman from Alabama, Chair of the House Foreign Affairs Committee.

Chairman William Fontroy had been a powerful force during the contentious Eighties, when foreign policy drew fierce battle lines on the Hill. But almost exactly coincident with the fall of the Cold War's most visible symbol, the Berlin Wall, old Billy Fontroy seemed to give up the fight. As free enterprisers rallied to sell off the graffiti-covered divider brick-by-brick, the Chairman started pulling up legislative stakes, shrugging off ancient disagreements, and generally checking out of Capitol life altogether.

Forgiving the pun, Billy had perhaps seen the proverbial writing on the wall. He foresaw the change coming. Ideological battle lines became *passé*, global economic domination stepped in as the only bone of contention. The transition might not have represented the end of history and the triumph of democracy; but, when money rose as the god to unite all *isms*, Billy lost his sense of fight. He wanted to retire. Yet when he tried to give up his seat, Party colleagues asked him to hold on for one more term. "Billy, old boy," they said, "we can't go losing that seat to the other side. We need your yellow hide right where it is."

Rick Peralta had made the most of this leadership vacuum. Chairman Fontroy was too detached to crack the whip. He hadn't even wanted to start work on reauthorizing the Foreign Assistance Act until after the next recess. Instead of spending time in his home district, he and his wife had planned to borrow the Beaufort, S.C., vacation home of a long-time acquaintance, whose advances in the field of agribusiness consistently led declines on Wall Street's futures market.

Billy had sought to stall his Committee's consideration of the omnibus legislation. Alas, Party leaders once again overruled him. Movement on the bill would be critical to fundraising efforts for dozens of reelection campaigns. "Billy, we got to maintain our majority," they said. So, there he sat, gavel in hand, Carolina on his mind.

Jaime had prepared six amendments for his boss to offer. Of the 5 related to Cuba, three had been drafted by CALB's attorneys. Jaime took some comfort in the fact that COG's report hadn't mentioned these, as the measures hadn't been run through the bipartisan Legislative Counsel office. The sixth amendment had to do with easing restrictions on the sale of certain high technology computer equipment to Pakistan. Non-proliferation goals were standing in the way of lucrative business for one of the largest employers in New Jersey. Peralta would be arguing that safeguards could effectively block any resale of the advanced hardware to third party nuclear aspirants and that an all- out prohibition was only hurting U.S. business and workers. Both this and the Cuba-related amendments would fall under Title IV of the bill. The Committee would be lucky to finish up Titles I and II by lunchtime. Peralta himself wouldn't even be attending the markup session due to scheduling conflicts. This was another reason for Jaime's flagging interest in the early proceedings. He used the time to mull over his afternoon challenges and the line-up for Title IV.

The Pakistan provision was a toss-up. It could go either way. The outcome didn't matter much. Peralta would come out looking like the champion for the folks back home either way. On the Cuba items, they had locked in the votes in Committee to pass some.

Two were to be pitched as "moderate" versions of the more far-reaching amendments that the COG report surfaced. These had been hastily repackaged in the hope of being passed off as compromise positions. The third, authorizing a switch in short and medium- wave signals to Cuba, would likely go unchallenged as a mere technical adjustment to current program activities. "We'll low-ball this one – call it a "technical correction to frequency channels. Members won't want to admit they don't understand the technology. It'll sail by easily," Peralta had joked. Jaime didn't really get the point either; but would be glad to secure another win for his boss.

Peralta was feeling good. Success in Committee seemed assured. The Miami scuffled hadn't rocked the boat. The outlook for passage on the House Floor was also looking promising. Santos and his team were holding up their end of the bargain with the Administration. All week, the President's people had been buttonholing key Members and twisting arms within the Caucus. "We need your vote to get those Florida delegates. The Party is finally making headway with the Miami crowd – if we can show them were on their side, they'll swing to our side on election day." Wishful thinking, perhaps, but even if the President couldn't win their votes, he'd at least pillage their pocketbooks.

ECHOS IN THE GARDEN

Ben O. Davey was a breakfast regular at the Old Ebbit Grill. Max, the headwaiter, greeted the Congressman and his guests warmly.

It's always a boon to have interesting, noteworthy personages frequent one's establishment. The smallest "About Town" blurb in *The Washington Post* can yield a fortnight's surge in business. Max hung close, in an effort to deduce whether the Congressman's entourage would be worth publicizing. It was a delicate balancing act. Max loitered up to the edge of discretion, yet he could determine little about the identities of the young woman, tall man, or the Congressman's distinguished-looking contemporary. Turning precisely, he politely returned to his post at the door. No food for the tattler this time, he concluded.

Forty-five minutes passed. The waiter delivered the check. Max had all but forgotten them. He would have been surprised indeed to know the true nature of their business and the details of the plan they'd just formulated. Tongues most certainly would have wagged.

Ben, Frank, Ada and Peter rose from the table, each with marching orders. They single-filed out onto 15th Street. The Old Ebbit stood yards from the White House, separated only by the stately structure housing the Department of the Treasury. Souvenir vendors and postcard stands littered the sidewalk. One door down in the opposition direction from Treasury was a more upscale source of Capital City memorabilia, a shop called *"Political Americana."* The store's window displayed a vast array of bumper stickers, presidential biographies, and photographs of the familiar faces of the nation's leaders past and present. Frank tapped his finger on the glass, pointing out a black and white portrait of William McKinley. "Platitudes for peace," he muttered derisively.

Ben stepped towards him. "Yes. One little amendment tacked onto the U.S. Army's appropriations bill...."

"...then grafted with impunity onto the Constitution of the sovereign isle of Cuba," Frank continued, shaking his head. "Independence gone from the get-go."

Ada shot Peter a puzzled look. "What are they're talking about?" she asked in a whisper.

Peter pointed at the grainy picture throughout the glass "Senator Platt carried an amendment for McKinley's administration. It ostensibly ended the U.S. military occupation of Cuba, which began during the Spanish-American war, but it basically gave America complete control of the island."

Frank must have overheard. Cutting in, "it was an annexation."

Ben nodded. *"What's past is prologue."*

FLEET FEET

Jaime shuffled through his in-box, discarding most of the contents, while munching a stale turkey club from the Rayburn cafeteria. He had roughly an hour before markup resumed and his boss was expected back in the office at any point. Jaime was using the time to refuel and regroup. He tossed the junk mail. Pertinent stuff was piled aside for reading later on.

Toss, toss, pile, toss, toss, toss... Jaime suspended this crude inventory, when he arrived at a curious looking, oddly shaped envelope. He tore at the edge, releasing the contents.

Glossy brochures spilled out, scattering dreamy images across his desk. Jaime picked one up. It featured tickertape send-off scenes, luxurious cabin interiors, and illustrations of sun-soaked revelry called forth. *FunShips: Find Your Fiesta Onboard!* The pamphlets cheered.

Jaime leaned back. Santos Cruise Lines. "No wonder that dude's so rich," he spoke aloud admiringly, "never misses the chance to sell a trip." Still smirking, he rose at the sound of the receptionist greeting Rick Peralta's return. Dropping the envelope in the bin, Jaime retrieved his mark-up folder from under the marketing materials and headed for a quick confab with the Congressman.

WATCHTOWER

The Hon. Ben O. Davey ducked into a quiet corridor and made his way up a discrete stairwell, which lead to a suite of rooms on the fifth floor of the Capitol Building. Few Members had access to this windowless region. Joe Public couldn't even get close. Armed policemen guarded the foot-thick, combination-locked steel doors behind which lie the operations of the House Permanent Select Committee on Intelligence or HPSCI (hip-see, phonetically).

This special committee is comprised of fewer than twenty Members of Congress, who've been appointed by the leaders of their respective parties to serve as the "eyes and ears" of their colleagues on matters of extreme sensitivity and national significance. In theory, HPSCI members have access to all the activities of the intelligence community. The Committee was established in 1977, to watchdog a Presidential Administration that had overstepped its bounds at home and abroad. One branch of government was acting to check the reach of another. This was oversight in theory, but new layers of secrecy in practice. Ben, a former HPSCI member, had spent a frustrating four terms trying to peel the onion's layers. The spooks he'd fought to make more accountable had mocked his fruitless efforts, covertly, of course.

Being a HPSCI alum did have its advantages, however. Ben knew the guards, the staff, and the correct procedures for gaining access to classified information. Raising as few warning flags as possible, he jotted down what he was looking for on the back of a phone message slip and winked at Judy the Committee's loyal gatekeeper. Judy imagined herself a bit of a Moneypenny, and she played favorites.

Ben, casual and flirtatious: "Oh, don't bother sending anything to my office; I don't have a safe there to secure papers. I can just browse through in one of the secured rooms here...less trouble that way. I'll only take a few minutes in any case, and besides, it gives me more time near you...." Waiting for her to blush, he lowered his voice just a touch: "I do miss you scolding me for being late to briefings," he winked. "Just leave a message with my secretary when the files have been brought down. I'll swing by for a peek and another visit."

And that was that. Now, he'd wait and silently thanked Brooke Glaze for knowing when and how to lead a horse to water. Lucky for both of them, Ben was hoping for something juicy to spill her way.

ALICE IN CHAINS

"Did Peter say when he'd be back?"

Rosie shook her head, "Sorry, honey, just waved a hand over his shoulder and hollered 'guard the fort' on his way out."

Ada's shoulders slumped.

"But you know," Rosie put in quickly, "he looked like a cat with a canary. Jazzed about something, that's for sure. And, in some kind of hurry."

Ada's eyes narrowed ever so slightly. "Did he talk with anyone before he left?"

"Took a call from Congressman Davey moments prior to departure."

"Really," Ada murmured thoughtfully. She caught Rosie cocking an eyebrow and imagined she could see the metaphorical equivalent of yellow feathers protruding from between her confidant's strong white teeth. "Rosie?" she coaxed.

"Yes, dear?"

Ada leaned across the older woman's desk, supplicant before innocent. "Did you happen to – oh, I dunno – catch any of what that conversation was about, accidentally, of course?"

"Well, now that you mention it. I did hear Peter laugh and exclaim: 'Bless that Brooke Glaze, I almost feel sorry for the spooks.'"

"Good ears!" Ada shook her head, "but what does it mean?"

"Got me, honey" Rosie shrugged.

Ada smiled, "I better get back to work, I guess."

"I'll let you know if he calls in."
"You're the tops, Rosie."
"Don't mention it, sugar."

THE MIGHTY QUINN

Ada sat down at the desk they placed for her in the corner of
Peter's office. Picking up the phone, she punched in Quinn's
number. Rusty fingers. The schoolmates hadn't spoken in over a
fortnight. That wasn't so unheard of. It's just that a lot had
transpired in those two weeks, much which couldn't be
communicated through fiber optics.

"Quinn Keegan, please."

"One moment. Who's calling, please?"

"Ada Tremont."

"With?"

"A friend," Ada replied, a little more curtly than she'd intended. It
took only a few seconds for Quinn to join the line.

"Hey stranger. Hear your trip was a wild ride."

"Yeah, Miami was…" she hesitated, "was it a topic of
conversation in your newsroom?"

"A bit outside our beat here." Quinn conceded what they both
already knew. "Dad was actually the one with the scoop. He's been
worried about you."

"Hmmm." Curiouser and curiouser.

"Well, that's the old man." Enough said. "Anyhow, what's up?"

"Do I need a reason to call?"

"No, but I'm sure you have one."

"Well," she laughed, "I actually do."

"Uh-huh. Lay it on me."

"You free for lunch?"

"I want a hint."

"Quinn, you take all the fun out of being circuitous."

"Thank you."

"A born reporter."

"For now."

"Okay," with a good-natured sigh, "The House is marking up the Foreign Assistance Act today, and I'm trying to get a hold of whatever press statements the Cuban American Liberation Bond will be putting out. Ideally, before they go out."

"And you thought I could help..."

"I thought if anyone could."

"Uh-huh."

"I know I'm asking a lot. This is important."

"I shouldn't, but I'll try for two reasons. One, Friday is my last day in this job. Two, I can't resist you."

"Wait. What? You're leaving. I thought you loved it there?"

"I do, as well as my family, as well as you – especially you – Ada. But I have to go. I'm not quitting this time. I got offered an overseas assignment. Once in a lifetime thing. Can't pass it up. I need this."

"More than me?"

"Ada," he let the silence hang. "We'll always be...how we are..."

"It was in the stars." She covered her hesitation with levity: "When an air sign meets another air sign, there is complete freedom of movement, little or no restriction. The blend can buoy the spirit or become stale without the winds of change."

"Ada..."

"What?"

"I love you."

"I love you too, Quinn."

"Still want to meet for lunch?"

"Please."

"I'll pick you up."

"Okay."

"I'll find what you're looking for."

Her voice straining, she whispered: "I miss you already, Quinn."

"Ditto, Ada."

TAPESTRY

Frank took back roads to avoid traffic on the Beltway. Maryland's pastoral pleasantries worked to regulate the speed of both his car and adrenaline level. No number of sleepy cows or silent cornfields, however, could sway his renewed sense of purpose. Having hopped back in the saddle, he wasn't about to get bucked, least of all by his own emotions. He should have taken a different exit, but knew he was riding solo now. Even his compatriots from back at the Old Ebbit Grill were to be spared prior knowledge of this secret mission.

Frank turned down an unmarked trail, leaving behind the quiet life of a retired civil servant. By the time he pulled up in front of the secluded cabin at the end of the road, the die was cast.

Frank took one look at the figure on the porch and concluded the coded directions had brought him to the right place. He stepped out of his car and extended a hand of greeting.

"Wayne."

The man nodded, looking off into the distance. Without meeting his eyes, he took Frank's hand in a brief clasp. "You better come in."

The cabin's interior proved an excellent approximation of the inhabitant's external appearance. Efficient ordered, anonymous. The large main room contained nothing beyond bare necessities. Agency training takes hold and doesn't let go. Frank shook the thought, remembering he was the one looking for a favor this time around.

"Your former partner was a good human being. Rare. I was sad to learn of his passing."

With an almost imperceptible bow of the head, the man spoke each word slowly: "It is a loss. He respected you too, Mr. Wayne. I will help you because of him."

Frank waited another moment, then described his request.

"Easily done."

"Excellent."

"Do you have the number with you? "

Frank did and gave it over along with a P.O. Box address.

Arrangements settled, they parted.

Chapter 7

SECOND TUESDAY 1996

"Glaze."

"Good morning."

Brooke recognized the electronically disguised voice of her mystery informant. "I appreciate you getting back in touch."

"I said I would call in one week. You can rely on me to keep my commitments. What have you learned since we last spoke?"

"Can we meet somewhere? I need more than just these brief conversations, if I'm to get anywhere with this."

"A meeting is not possible."

"I can arrange for it to be totally secret. I needn't even see your face. I just want more than two minutes of your time."

"We are approaching that limit now."

"I realize that, but at this point it doesn't matter. My investigation is stalled by a lack of hard leads. I believe you when tell me you've got the goods on Santos. I do. In fact, I now think you're the only one who can really open this up. Hints here and there just aren't panning out, however. I need your help to get him."

"You ought not to underestimate yourself, Ms. Glaze, I certainly don't. In fact, I believe you may just be trying to tempt me out of the shadows with these expressions of defeat. That is fine, I understand. But I cannot come to you. Not now, at least. You will receive something in the post this afternoon. I hope you will use it. Travel is said to open new vistas. Good-bye, Ms. Glaze, and bon voyage."

NO SIMPLE HIGHWAY

He took her to the waterfront. They watched the Potomac's lazy traffic drift by. Kayaks carved thin vanishing patterns. A Georgetown crew team stroked the surface at a common pace. Alee, the Kennedy Center's brass and stone facade shone forth. Across the water, Theodore Roosevelt island lay in repose. To starboard, the river vanished back to its source, bounding the path of the famed Freedom Trail's last leg, the C&O Canal.

Ada and Quinn dangled their feet off the pier, recollecting old times, old plans, old dreams. The sun slipped beneath the horizon and the scene grew still. Twinkling lights from the nearby dockside bar, SEQUOIA, winked coyly in their direction. They succumbed. After a couple pints of Anchor Steam, the friends, by mutual consent, opted to skip dinner and return home to Quinn's apartment to say good-bye.

They made a very different kind of love. Reverence replaced laughter, and they clung to each other with the dull throb of loss. They did not know what they would be to each other in the future, but both knew that romance would never feel as carefree or as simple again. They weren't kids anymore.

Ada rose and went to the bathroom. When she emerged, Quinn was leaning over the bed extracting something from a crumpled pool of garments. His trouser pocket yielded two sheets of paper. He handed them to her.

"Advance drafts of the Cabal's press release."

She couldn't help but smile. How like Quinn to wait until after. Taking the pages, she scanned them quickly.

"Any surprises?" he prompted.

"I'm not sure," Ada answered pensively, rereading a third time, "there's an odd sort of scant mention of a broadcasting amendment." She looked up with an almost imperceptible squint.

Quinn shrugged, "maybe too technical to make it a big deal."

Squinting more noticeably now, Ada returned her attention to the papers in her hand. "Yeah," she mumbled without conviction. "And yet...these guys try to take credit for everything – the moon over Miami, humidity in Havana. It's much more their style to puff up a small success and parade it around. Santos never misses an opportunity to boast. They could have found some way to make the amendment sexier for the media." She tapped her front tooth with the puzzling press release, "if they'd wanted to."

Sensing her thoughts withdraw, anticipating the physical counterpart, Quinn began to dress. She followed.

"Hey, Ada," he asked, "will you come by here next week, check on the place, bring in any mail. I've canceled my subscriptions and left a forwarding address with the Post Office, but sometimes it takes a while for that stuff to take effect."

"No problem. I still have my set of keys." She stopped and looked down.

He shook his head. Grinning, "worried they've rusted with neglect in the past couple weeks?"

She grinned back, "Very funny." Then she threw her arms around him, squeezing tight.

PLOWSHARE

Peter began to pace the floor. Eagerness propelled him. Ben was due back at any moment, perhaps bearing juicy forbidden fruits from his harvest in the fields of the shadow world. The two had been deep in scenario spinning when the call from the ersatz Miss Moneypenny came in. The documents that the Congressman requested access to that morning would be held for his review in a secured room in the HPSCI offices. They exchanged thumbs-up and Ben sped off. That was nearly two hours ago.

Peter chuckled to himself, hoping that the delay reflected the wealth of material to be absorbed and not some sort of run in with a colleague wondering why Ben was poking around. He could tell immediately, however, from the look on the face of the returning distinguished gentleman from Massachusetts, that the former was the case. And a smug mug it was. Triumph shone forth from the corners of Ben's cherubic cheeks.

"B-I-N-G-O?"

"As close as it gets," Ben rejoined.

"Spell it out for me?"

"Of course, my young friend, all in good time. Pour us a drop of that nectar, first" he said, gesturing pointedly and nodding approvingly, as Peter did so. "Ah, fine, yes, that loosens the vocal cords."

Peter took a sip as well. They both reclined on the standard 6-foot leather couches issued – choice of black, red or blue – to all

Members of Congress for use in their offices. Peter stretched his long legs before him. Ben too slid down to a more relaxed angle, propping his feet up on an unmistakably non-regulation calico-covered, donkey-shaped, union-labeled stool, which had been a gift from the elite (in numbers, if not in notoriety) West Roxbury Democratic Women's Community Action League and Sewing Circle. Thus settled, Ben broke his oath to preserve and protect Uncle Sam's secrets. He made Peter privy to classified material – data unknown, unimagined, and (in this cynical age, perhaps) uninteresting to the American populace at large. Ben's was hardly a precedent-setting leak. Just a personal rather than a historical first.

Ben's request had been relatively vague: 1) so as not to attract attention and, consequently, refusal by either the agency personnel or Intel Committee staff; and 2) because he didn't really know what he was looking for, hence making the "wide net" approach all the more appropriate. He'd simply asked for the year-to-date records on traffic, human and otherwise, between Cuba and the United States, which was classified at or above the level of "secret." This is just a side comment, but there's something about government officials that makes them want to give a special classification label for everything remotely sensitive. As a country, we've ended up with a fatuous array of rubber stamps. Classification levels say: "off limits to John Q. Public" in escalating ways, such as "secret," "top secret," "restricted," "closed access," "authorized only," and "code black," to name a few.

At any event, the upshot of Ben's netting venture in the seas and skies of the southern Atlantic was a rather tantalizing hint at a larger, more intriguing puzzle. New questions meant their probe could gain direction and force. The biggest mystery to emerge from Ben's blind stab was this: in the past nine months, over a dozen members of the Cuban air force had defected to the United States by flying their Soviet-era fighter planes to a naval station near Key West, Florida. This was big news. Yes? A huge embarrassment for Castro, a victory for U.S. policy, right? Seems like the perfect publicity coup for a group like CALB that was, according to the intelligence reports, involved in helping repatriate these defectors. And yet, nary a one of these MiG-21 jet landings was reported. A tight news lock on each of these incidents had been imposed and maintained. In fact, in one instance, deliberately misleading information was given in response to inquiries from a local reporter, acting on a tip from a curious fisherman in the area, who'd alleged suspicious activity at the naval base.

The classified reports did not suggest any national security rationale for keeping these defections under wraps. There was no mention of attempts to elicit valuable revelations about military maneuvers or the political climate back in Cuba from the captured pilots. Their interrogations had been strictly *pro forma*. What's more, the pilots were clearly not spies working for the United States, whose identities needed to be protected. In fact, the case files were so thin on substance that the tedium under which they were conducted was almost palpable. It was as though each cursory conclusion was punctuated by the reporting investigator's apathetic yawn.

The only thing these defection incidents might be good for was a lot of noisy horn tooting and flag waiving of the sort the Cuban American Liberation Bond had a more than passing familiarly. The fleeing pilot's stories were tailor-made for a self-promotional publicity circus ala-Cabal. If they could draw hundreds to the streets of Miami's Little Havana to welcome Cuban everyman rafters freshly fished and still soggy from their ocean crossings to freedom's shores, just think of the turn-out they might garner by showcasing real-life examples of Fidel's crumbling defenses. None of this made sense.

Ben and Peter sought to puzzle out the logic; but hit a dead end. Some other principle must be at play. Something was operating like a magnet beneath the table, guiding the players on the board to make counterintuitive moves. The best way to unearth such a hidden force, Ben figured, was to identify who might have activated the magnet in the first place. Or, failing that, figure out which if any of the figures involved might be persuaded to break their silence and speak their own suspicions.

WALKING BACK THE CAT

"I figured you were with Ben when you disappeared yesterday," Ada was saying, "was Frank with you too?"

"No, we left him a couple of messages, but never heard back. Come to think of it, I still have yet to speak with him," Peter reflected, then returned to the matter at hand: the spreading of Ben's security leak one concentric ring further by sharing it with his sidekick.

She listened intently as he put forth findings and theories concerning the secret MIG-21 defections. Eyes narrowed and speculative, she tapped out a brief riff on the corner of Peter's desk.

"Hang on a sec'," she said moving to her own desk to retrieve CALB's embargoed press statement, the one Quinn had obtained for her. "Tell me what you make of this."

When he'd read it, Peter looked up at her, a twinkle in his eye. "Where'd you get a hold of this?"

Anxious to make her point, she ignored the question, so much less pertinent than the one she'd hoped for. "But didn't you notice, Peter, there's just one bland mention of Peralta's broadcasting amendment? He's obsessed with propaganda programs. Frank told me all about the video games and other ploys." She continued rather breathlessly, "Maybe it's nothing, but I had the same reaction as you and Ben did to the defection thing. Why are Santos and the Cabal so greedy for coverage of some successes and so uncharacteristically understated or discrete about others?"

"Why indeed. To know that would be to know the game they're

121

really playing. Before we get to that, though, will you tell me how you managed to wheedle this out of CALB before the mark-up is even over?"

"I asked a friend for help. He got it for me."

"Do you know how?"

"I didn't ask, exactly. But he's a reporter, so I thought it'd be easier for him, you know, to pretend he was doing preliminary inquiries or something."

"Yeah, well normally it would be, but CALB's press office is very tightly run. Nothing is supposed to go out without approval from Santos. You know how paranoid they are over there. I just wondered if there was a higher connection."

Ada was starting to feel uncomfortable, not to mention disappointed. "I don't know what to say, I thought it'd be helpful for us, I hope I didn't do anything wrong."

"Oh, damn, Ada. Sorry, I'm not giving you a hard time. It's very helpful. Awesome, actually. I'm just...I guess I'm just shocked your pal was able to get a hold of it. It's um...impressive...very."

Ada blushed. "He's creative. And connected, I guess." she ventured. "

"Let's hope his good fortune holds out. I'd hate to think of Santos' reaction if he discovers this breech in security."

"Well, you know, it's really not an issue anymore," she said, working to regain composure, "he's left the country on assignment, so Santos couldn't find him if he tried."

Not a complete Neanderthal, Peter let the subject drop. He knew a line when he'd tripped over it, so he backpedaled, returning to Ada's original point about the curious omission. They continued discussing Ben's discoveries, trying to approach the maze from different angles. After a half-hour of back-and-forth theory testing, they found themselves recircling the same ground.

Ada sighed. "I'm not sure were getting anywhere, Peter."
"Fresh perspective, that's what we need, something to reboot our thought patterns."

"We need to run it by the Oracle himself. Let's figure out where he's disappeared to?"

"Let's."

They rose and went off in search of Frank.

COCKNEY CLUES

Even though the phone had rung without answer, Frank's place still seemed the best place to start looking for clues on where he might have gone.

The pair shared a pleasant ride from COG's offices to Georgetown. Peter, always more relaxed when outdoors, whistled tunes and told stories to keep Ada entertained. He apparently had an anecdote to match nearly every point of interest along the way; some were personal stories from his younger days in D.C. and others involved famous figures who'd left a mark on America's Capital City.

Ada nodded along and tried not to think about how much she liked the sound of his voice.

Peter turned off the motor and walked round to open her door. Ada was already out of the car by the time he got there.

"Lancelot! I'm too anxious."

"Ha. You go."

Peter gestured for her to precede him up the path to the front entrance. When they reached the door, Peter pressed the button.

The imposing gong resounded, but no footsteps arrived.

"Not a creature was stirring," Peter declared.

Ada peered through the darkened window of the sitting room. "Looks pretty empty. No signs of recent puttering. Should we check if the car is gone? Look for a note or something?"

They poked about, turned up nothing, and went back to where they started.

Staring at the front door, Peter pursed his lips and let his eyes roam the brick frontage. "This a long shot," he eyed her tentatively, "and I'll need some help. You're going to have to sit on my shoulders."

"You must be joking." He shook his head.

"All aboard," Peter teased, as he crouched down and helped Ada climb on.

"Now what?"

"Run your hand along the transom, way to the far back, where the shelf hits the brickwork."

"Can you move a little closer."

Peter pressed closer to the door and stretched up on his toes. "Feel anything?"

"I, I think so. Can you boost me up just a little more? I can't quite reach." A brief partnership of stretching and hopping did the trick: "Got it! Feels like paper." Back on level ground, she held it out but kept her grip on the envelope she'd just retrieved: "How did you know there'd be something there?"

"A guess, really. Just looking at the house from the outside again brought me back to the first time I met Frank, the only time actually, before my parents died. It was a short visit. I must have been ten or eleven. I took the train from boarding school to meet my folks. They were in Washington for a night. We all stayed here. I think Frank felt bad for me because my parents were off at meetings the whole time. He kept me entertained by playing spy games. He invented a hiding place, "a drop," that only I was light enough to reach. He taught me to jump up and grab the ledge above the door, then by pulling, I could hook my elbow on for long enough to sweep my other hand around, looking for a coded message. Then, he taught me the trick to rhyming cockney slang, so we could communicate in riddles."

"Incredible."

"Yeah. I'd almost forgotten...wild that he should remember. Well," Peter concluded hastily "I'm not light enough to swing myself up there anymore. He must have known you'd be with me. What say we examine the message you discovered?"

He held it out so they could both see the note.

"The President's Gay and Frisky" Ada looked up: "Is this humor?"

124

"If I'm not mistaken, it's a clue," Peter winked, "station one of a scavenger hunt." Clearly relishing the mystery: "Shall we work through the clues at the designated watering hole?"

She opened her mouth to speak, then shut it. I shouldn't spoil his fun, she reasoned, he'll tell me soon enough. "Lead on."

Peter drew Ada's arm through his and led her down the path to the car. This time, she waited for him to open the door before reclaiming the passenger side.

Across the street from a porch swing carved by her dear Harry over a decade ago, an 88-year-old widow, mother of four, grandmother of nine, gave a long sigh of satisfaction. She hadn't any idea why the nice young couple was calling upon her nice neighbor; too bad he wasn't around to receive them. Not that they seemed to mind, playing around like acrobats. It was fun to watch their high jinks. Oh, for those days again. To be young and flirtatious, without a worry in the world.

OCCIDENTALLY ON PURPOSE

Peter deposited his keys into the dove gray gloves of the parking attendant and proceeded up the carpet crested with the Willard Hotel insignia. This splendidly rendered example of Beaux-Arts architecture loomed formidably from its prestigious Pennsylvania Avenue perch on the site of the original six dilapidated structures purchased by Henry Willard in 1847, for which the Supreme Court had ruled he must pay in gold coin rather than paper money.

A mere block away from the White House itself, the now-grand hotel had catered to generations of VIP visitors.

Back in tour-giving mode, Peter illustrated this point by recounting that President Lincoln himself had been in the habit of stealing away to the Willard's plush, but discreetly configured lobby, to snatch precious moments of privacy. There, he had been able to read and think without the constant interruptions of his official office at the White House. Abe's secret retreat didn't remain so for long, however. The brasher supplicants simply began to stalk the President, cornering him in a wingback chair, right there in the Willard's lobby.

"Lobbyists?" Ada queried.

"Birthplace of a breed."

"Is this the watering hole you mentioned?"

"No, it's just a stop on tour – one more yarn for your collection. Plus, they have valet." He gave her a quick glance. "Right, then, westward ho. Next door."

A few minutes later, they stepped through the doors of the Occidental Grill. The entrance way was decorated with oil paintings of 20th Century Presidents, while black and white photographs of movers and shakers, heroes and heroines lined the restaurant's walls. Ada identified as many faces as she could, as Peter guided her up the brass stairwell to the second floor: George C. Marshall, Adlai Stevenson, Neil Armstrong, Edward R. Murrow, Susan B. Anthony, Charles Lindberg, Janet Rankin.

"Resonant."

Ada nodded in agreement. "Wasn't that the bar downstairs, Peter?" she asked pointing back over the railing.

"That's the main bar. I'm taking you to the Truman Room." He walked her towards the rear of the building. As they stepped closer, Ada began to hear a livelier set of voices. The scent of cigars grew unmistakable. She had a vision of the scene in her mind before the real thing loomed larger than life and stranger than fiction.

"What are we drinking?" Ada quipped, as they approached the bar, "Papa Dobles?"

A voice chimed in, "If I'm not mistaken, your friend will be having a straight shot of ole Kentucky."

Peter turned to the speaker, a man of ageless majesty. Impressively broad shouldered with wavy locks, his periwinkle blue eyes pierced the aromatic haze.

"I.W. Harper's the ticket," Peter confirmed, "but only if you'll join us."

The man conveyed his approval with an expression so devilishly charming that Ada imagined she heard the echo of angels weeping.

He called to the bartender: "Collin, look who's come to see us. And with a companion immeasurably more attractive than that suspect character with whom he's been spotted on previous occasions."

Reaching over the bar to shake hands, "Hullo, Peter. Good to have you by," he said warmly. "And would your guest like an I.W. Harper's as well?"

"You'll have a bourbon with us, won't you, Ada?"

"Certainly," she replied, turning towards the man to whom she'd not yet been introduced. "I'm Ada Tremont, by the way."

"I'm sorry," Peter said quickly, "Daniel Bell, this is my colleague, Ada Tremont. Ada, meet Danny, Frank's oldest, blithest friend. You'd be advised to keep a firm grip on your heartstrings, legend has it, he's irresistible."

"You might extend to me the same advice," rejoined Danny Bell, as he cast another smile in Ada's direction.

Ada blushed, her sympathy for the lamenting angels increasing. "I can see how you and Frank would be well-suited," she commented, repressing the urge to flash him a winsome grin.

Peter intervened. "Ah, then, you two, to what shall we drink?"

"To the President."

"The President?" Ada raised a quizzical eye.

"Mr. Truman. We're in his bar, drinking his favorite whiskey." Peter added: "He used to keep a private stash in his bathroom. Bess apparently never even knew."

Ada lifted the glass to her lips. "To the man from Missouri."

"To Give 'em Hell Harry."

"To I.W. Harper's, the President's Gay and Frisky."

Ada caught the men exchange a look, then Danny remove a small envelope from inside his jacket. He set it on the bar and shook Peter's hand, "Thanks for the drink. Let's have another before too long." Turning to Ada, "with true respect," was all he said as he left them.

The pressure of Peter's fingers on her arm silenced Ada. Peter guided her to a set of velvet chesterfields at the far corner of the room. There ensconced in the chair's sheltering wings, Peter drew out the envelope Danny had passed him. They moved their heads even closer together and examined the contents.

bath,

leaky dog scaper brussel sorry pitch 'apenny bat o'wed sobe butcher's dinkey doo x clickety click badger's frog

- china

"Looks like Jabberwocky," Ada confessed.

"Right country, wrong class," Peter said lightly. "It's rhyming slang from the east end of London, invented to outwit eavesdroppers and agents of the law."

"Are you going to initiate me into the mysteries of Cockney?"

"I'll hit for a rabbit!" he teased.

Suspicious, but at a loss for clues, she crossed her arms, warning him from astride the forked path between jest and vexation: "are you pulling my leg?"

"Your leg, as in your *scotch*. You see the phrase *scotch peg* rhymes with 'leg.' Cockney would shorten the phrase by dropping the sounds-like part, so leg becomes scotch. Follow me?"

"I suppose so. That's not the first rhyme that would have popped into my head, though. What's a peg anyhow?"

"A peg's basically a shot of whatever you're drinking. But yes, these aren't today's expressions. But, if you'd been born in and around the sounds of Bow Bells (a.k.a., St. Mary-le-Bow Church), in 18th Century London, the terms would be part of the banter."

"True enough, I suppose."

"By the way, if you want to say something popped into your head, it's *loaf*, as in *bread loaf.*

"Peter..."

"Right, let's have a crack at this puzzle then." Peter spread the short note out before them. "Got a pen?"

She dug through her bag. "Sorry," she said, handing him a clear plastic implement filled with glitter and a vessel that could at a distance have been mistaken for a submarine. At close range, however, it actually suggested a racier ride. "My friend just got engaged – it was a party favor. You know, a bachelorette sendoff...Oh, never mind! Let's just get started. It works, at least."

"I would hope so." Peter dead panned.

Aware that by now her complexion must fairly match the room's rich magenta and cherry wood furnishings, Ada threw her hands up. "Tease away."

Peter raised his brow but held his tongue. He turned his attention back to the coded message before them.

Ada remained quiet as he dissected, distinguishing between recognizable cockney and as yet unidentifiable connectors.

bath bun	son or sun
leaky	?
dog and bone	phone
scapa flow	go away quickly
brussel sprout	scout
sorry and sad	bad

pitch and toss	boss
'a penny dip	ship
bat and wicket	ticket
wed	?
sobe	?
butcher's hook	look
dinkey doo	twenty-two
x	?
clickety click	sixty-six
badger's	?
frog and toad	road
china plate	mate

    "Let's assume," Peter began, after studying the crib sheet for some moments, "that he's beginning with a salutation and ending with a signature. That gives us a message to "son," that's me, signed by "mate," that'd be Frank."

    "Makes sense. What about the rest?"

    "I can't get all the words, but I think he's sort of mixing clues in with rhyming slang words, so we'll have to extrapolate to find the sense. Alright, next comes 'leaky' then 'phone' -- leaks in phones sound like tapped lines to me. Then there's a longer string which together seem to form a semi-complete statement: "go away quickly scout bad boss ship."

    "Bad boss ship? Santos' Fiesta floats?"

    "Yes," Peter smiled. "Okay, 'ticket' maybe that's the ticket he took to scout out the ship...but what's 'wed'?"

    "If 'wed' and 'sobe' aren't cockney, then perhaps we should consider them more modern shortenings." She paused to determine whether or not she was being taken seriously.

    Peter was nodding encouragement, "keep going."

    "How about 'wed' for Wednesday and 'sobe' for South Beach -- there's a big cruise ship port there. We kept driving past it."

    "Excellent."

    "Let's do the second line."

    "Second line, right. Start by noting for the record that it could mean this is a new part of the message. He had space just to continue on and run it all together. But we could be reading too much into it. Anyhow, duly noted."

"Check."

"The string goes: 'look twenty-two x sixty-six badger's road'. Oh damn," Peter spoke still in a hushed tone, "I almost forgot." He pulled a small brass key from his pant pocket. "This was on the cocktail napkin when Collin handed me my drink – oh, by the way, whiskey as in *gay and frisky*, the clue directing us to the Truman room. That's Frank spreading the bases."

Impatiently. "But what's it a key to? It's so small."

"The identifying marks have been scratched off, but I'd wager it fits a post office box on Wisconsin "the Badger State" Avenue. Multiply 22 by 66 and we can try box number 1456."

"Unreal."

"Over the top?"

"It just seems a lot of complication just to convey some information and ask for a favor."

"That may be. But don't forget the first item in Frank's note. The reason he didn't just call us is that he doesn't trust the phones."

ANYTHING GOES

In olden days a glimpse of stocking
Was looked on as something shocking

The queue writhed like a python stuffed with mice. Its constituent assembly was comprised of senior citizens anxious to make their dream vacations come true; newlyweds itching for a box spring mattress; and short-fused parents desperate to deposit their insolent progeny in a separate room. The Santos Cruise Company's Fiesta Line had particularly monopolized the field of family entertainment. This distinction had little to do with the respective wholesomeness of the activities available. Virtually all packaged holiday cruise companies offered a comparable mix of casinos, nightclubs, adults-only pools, spas and other over-21 adventure alternatives. It was Santos Fiesta Cruise Lines, however, that recognized adults would play twice as hard – and pay twice as much – to have their kids kept elsewhere occupied while they did so. On a Fiesta ship, Mom and Dad indulged, while little Dave and Tammy were distracted with shuffleboard, arcade games, and sundry other age- specific endeavors.

Given this, the hoard boarding the Fiesta FunShip had a definite suburban family feel to it. Any stray single stood out. A male of this scarce breed had in fact already identified a female counterpart and was eyeing her with marked interest. The solo woman under watch was advancing beyond the reception post, moving swiftly deeper into the belly of the boat.

Her hunter pushed ahead in hasty pursuit. Drat! As bad luck would have it, his advance was blocked by a considerably more buxom Cruise Director than the Julie McCoy of *Love Boat* TV show fame. This hospitality stewardess, a veritable Valkyrie, stood firm, with clipboard upraised and preparing to do battle against on-board apathy. She blazed her brightest beam towards the sexy-in-a-grandfatherly-kind-of-way man straining impatient eyes over her shoulder.

"A little to the left, sailor, you might find the view more pleasing," she coaxed almost like she meant it.

"Dear," the man responded, "if you'd be so good as to give me my key and cabin number."

"You'll need to get that from the purser, Andy, over there," she indicated with a tilt of her shoulder, "I'm here to put the fun in your FunShip experience!" Studying her clipboard, "We have all sorts of things to keep our guests happy. Like, we have..."

"I'm quite sure you're full of intriguing ideas, but I assure you, I really must find my room immediately." He craned to catch the purser's attention.

Confused, sensing she might have done or said something wrong, she held his arm, "Are you sure? Wouldn't you like me to suggest something? You mustn't stay in your room, you know, mingling is all part of the fiesta flow," she insisted.

"Tell you what, why don't you choose my fun. I'm in your hands. The name is C.O. Jones," he said with a bow.

Reflecting pride and vindication, she curtsied in return. "You're a good sport, Mr. Jones. I'll make your selections now. I promise, you'll thank me for this. "

"I don't doubt that for an instant."

The purser proved as well suited to his responsibilities as the Cruise Director was to hers. With an accommodating nod, Andy extended a general information package and specific directions without delay.

"Welcome aboard, Mr. Jones. Here's the key to your stateroom. The fastest way is to go up the main stairs, turn left and take the first set of elevators to the Hibiscus deck. You're in number 505."

Passenger Jones knew the odds were against his catching a better look at the woman from the queue; she carried herself with the distinct air of a non-dawdler. Nonetheless, he gave fate the benefit of the doubt and charged up the garishly carpeted staircase like a sheriff's deputy on a bordello raid. "Damn," he muttered out of breath at the top, "lost her." He mustered a philosophical sigh, assumed a more leisurely pace, and took a leeward turn. Waiting for the elevator, he considered the likelihood of a correct identification. Was it really her? He'd only seen her photo from time to time; usually in a group shot, earnest faces gathered around the table at some charity event. Even in those settings, she stood out as focused and formidable.

Unlike the masses of cruise-goers boarding the FunShip to frolic, relax, gamble, or party on open seas and in loose ports, this woman looked all business, even in short shorts, strappy sandals and a Chicago Bulls cap.

BOOTLEG

"Do you think he's in trouble?"

"No," Peter answered slowly, "just cautious."

"Why does he think his phones are tapped?"

"Maybe this will tell us something." Peter extracted the contents of mailbox 1456. He looked over his shoulder. They were alone, except for a postal clerk, whose view was obscured by the angle of the wall. "Slip that in your bag," he whispered, pressing the envelop to her chest. "We'll open it at home."

She gave him a funny look.

Once inside the confines of his car, she exhaled the breath she'd been holding: "You know, I wouldn't put it past you and Frank to concoct an elaborate ruse just for the thrill of it."

"You disapprove of adventure?"

"I'm riding shotgun, am I not?" she countered.

"That's the spirit!"

The drive from the Wisconsin Avenue postal branch in Glover Park to Peter's U Street digs took less than ten minutes. He gave Ada keys to let herself in and drove around the corner in search of parking. She hadn't been back since that first visit, right before they'd left for Miami. It seemed ages ago. She suppressed the desire to poke about and passed the time by flipping on some downstairs lights. The one liberty that she did take was to open a couple of beers. Music, she considered, might not be appropriate.

She settled in on the smaller couch and took a pull of ale,

jumping up moments later at the sound of Peter's knuckles on the door.

"Hey," she said by way of greeting, "found a spot?"

"Yeah, not too far away."

"I opened a beer for you."

"Perfect, let's get to it."

"Here."

Peter studied the envelop then dug a finger beneath the flap and along the edge. A small cassette tape fell out into his hand.

"Do you have something to play that on?"

From an old roll top desk, Peter removed a mini recorder of the type favored by field reporters. He popped in the tape and pushed play. For a few moments, they heard only scratchy static and an occasional pop. Then, the sound of a phone line being engaged. A woman picked up on the first ring. The conversation was relatively short. The other voice sounded unnatural, as though filtered through a distortion device. The dialog was clear as a bell. Less apparent, was who had sent the tape to Frank's mailbox and how the recording had been obtained in the first place.

Peter rewound and played it again, this time transcribing into a notebook:

"Glaze."

"Good morning."

"I appreciate you getting back in touch."

"I said I would call in one week. You can rely on me to keep my commitments. What have you learned since we last spoke?"

"Can we meet somewhere? I need more than just these brief conversations if I'm to get anywhere with this."

"A meeting is not possible."

"I can arrange for it to be totally secret. I needn't even see your face. I just want more than two minutes of your time."

"We are approaching that limit now."

"I realize that, but at this point it doesn't matter. My investigation is stalled by a lack of hard leads. I believe you when tell me you've got the goods on Santos. I do. In fact, I now think you're the only one who can really open this up. Hints here and there just aren't panning out, however. I need your help to get him."

"You ought not to underestimate yourself, Ms. Glaze, I certainly don't. In fact, I believe you may just be trying to tempt me out of the shadows with these expressions of defeat. That is fine, I understand. But I cannot come to you. Not now, at least. You will receive something in the post this afternoon. I hope you will use it. Travel is said to open new vistas. Good-bye, Ms. Glaze, and bon voyage."

"Bon voyage? Sea air? Are you thinking what I'm thinking?"

"That Frank's got company. Yeah, whether he knows it or not."

"What do you mean? Don't you figure that's why he ran off in such a hurry and booked onto a cruise...to tail Brooke Glaze?" Ada ventured.

"Possible," Peter seemed to be concentrating.

Not wanting to interrupt for answers, Ada tried to trace his logic. Illumination dawned as she stared at the now-empty envelope. I'm getting better at this, she thought to herself. "Possible, but not likely," she reasoned aloud, "because we seem to be the first recipients of this tape. It's been post marked with today's date, so it had to have been mailed from close by, maybe even the same branch. So, either Frank had someone else send it after listening himself or Frank wanted us to pick up a delivery that he knew he wouldn't be here to collect himself. "

Peter smiled, "Exactly my thoughts."

Ada had peeled away the label on her beer bottle. She sneaked a peek in his direction. He looked not at her fidgety hands but directly into her eyes. She tried blinking to break the lock, yet it held, so she stared back. Peter rose and moved next to her on the couch.

"Ada, what's on your mind?"

"I feel like Alice in Wonderland."

"The only sane creature in a world of nonsense and fantasy?"

She laughed. "Red queen to white knight?"

Peter slid his arm around her waist and drew her closer. Her hair hung about his face. She could feel the pressure of his hands against her ribcage, felt the quick beat of her heart from within. She broke into her best Cheshire cat grin and began to kiss him lightly on the lips.

"Sweet mercy!" The phone jangled to life and broke the spell.

"You'd better get it."

Peter stumbled towards the offending appliance. "Hello."

"Peter. It's Ben. Hope I haven't called at a bad time?"

Peter gazed over at Ada. "No problem. We need to meet."

"That's why I'm calling. Can you join me tomorrow for breakfast?"

"We can."

"Okay. Old Ebbits at eight."

Chapter 8

SECOND WEEKEND 1996

"This is Brooke Glaze. I'm out of the office on assignment this week. Leave a message and I'll return it next Monday. If you need to reach me urgently, please press zero and ask to speak with Paul Towers."

The caller did not press zero. The caller put the receiver down with a look of satisfaction. Technology had provided the desired confirmation. All was proceeding according to plan.

THE DOTTED LINE

The man's entry cast a temporary ray of sunlight across the dark lounge interior. The doors swung shut and he stood waiting for his vision to adapt, letting his senses luxuriate in the cool stillness and the low pitch of a solitary voice accompanied by piano.

> *My story is much too sad to be told.*
> *But practically everything leaves me totally cold.*
> *The only exception I know is the case*
> *When I'm out on a quiet spree*
> *Fighting vainly the old ennui*
> *And suddenly turn and see...*

True to Cole Porter's promise, hers was the first face he saw when his eyes adjusted. The instincts of the man registered as C.O. Jones had been doubly right. Not only was he now certain that the lone figure at the bar was the woman he'd before only seen in photos. He'd also supposed correctly that she would avoid the send-off mixer on the Calypso deck for a quieter spot.

He took a seat.

The barman placed a napkin down before to his new customer. "Something I can get you, sir?"

"Bombay martini. Dry."

"Very good, sir." He held the customer's gaze. Good guess, the bartender seemed to be communicating. The lady a seat away was having the same.

Our man leaned back, waiting for his drink. He took the matchbook from the ashtray in front of him, seeming to study the *Fiesta Line* logo. "Need a light," he asked without looking up.

The woman cast a sidelong glance and gave the inquirer a swift survey. "A light?" she wondered. The man looked respectable, no manifest signs of lechery. Looks could be deceiving; that she knew. Nonetheless, she considered herself a skilled reader of people. She had to be. This guy was registering low on the bullshit meter. Plus, she still wasn't exactly sure what she was supposed to be doing on board this cruise. Maybe he had a message from her mysterious caller. So, rather than ignore him, she turned slightly, "a light?" she repeated.

He gestured towards the unlit cigarette she held scissored between her index and middle fingers.

She looked down. "No, thank you." She'd forgotten it was there.

Emboldened by the arrival of his cocktail, he pressed on. "I don't mean to disturb, but we seem to be the only two castaways not attending the welcoming party. Would you indulge an old man's curiosity?"

"Proceed," she answered with good-natured caution.

"The unlit cigarette?"

"Three guesses."

"The cigarette is a tool to facilitate mental exercise. You practice object bending, levitation, and spontaneous combustion." He tried to look earnest.

"Strike one," she responded skeptically, "though I'm not sure that shouldn't count as three attempts."

"I think we can rule our indecision, as well as posturing," he reasoned aloud. Snapping his fingers: "Alright. I'll forgo the third guess, if you give me double or nothing odds. Let me buy you a drink if I score a hit with pitch number two?"

"Irregular; but go ahead."

Assuming the pompous air of Sherlock Holmes, he made the following diagnosis: "You have given up the habit. Abandoning nicotine was the easy part. Losing the physical feel of a cigarette's presence in your hand has been tougher. You miss the tactile comfort, the delicate balance, the point of emphasis it provides."

She surrendered a shrug. "If a child doesn't have to lose a digit to give up thumb-sucking, then why must I drop this appendage?

"Commendable." He signaled for another martini for her. The barman sallied forth with the spoils. "To your harmless habit and your gracious indulgence, Miss…?"

"Lazar, she hesitated, Dolores Lazar."

"Ah, Dolores Lazar," he repeated, watching her steadily.

She took a sip. An alias is an alias; she'd used them before. Only thing different this time was that she hadn't chosen it herself. False names should be basic, nondescript, and forgettable. She shook her head, remembering a sacred rule from grade school talent shows, always pick your own routine. This man gave her the uncomfortable sensation that he could read her mind. Pushing her short hair back behind her ears and straightening her posture, she settled an easy smile on her lips then pinned him with her eyes. Now, I'm going to turn the tables, she said to herself.

Any lingering doubts about her identity were blown away by that look. It didn't matter what name she offered; he was certain now. This woman was not Dolores Lazar.

"How very *allusive*," he said with a waggish grin. She held her stare, but raised an eyebrow to communicate an unspoken, "oh?"

"You'll have to excuse me; I just have Nabokov on the brain. A friend was telling me she'd been named after one of his characters. I'm now remembering that wonderful passage." He quoted: *She was Lo, plain Lo, in the morning, standing four feet ten in one sock. She was Lola in slacks. She was Dolly at school. She was Dolores on the dotted line. But in my arms she was always Lolita.*

"How old is this friend of yours?"

Frank blushed in spite of himself. "Ha."

"Some find it a depressing name. Dolores."

"Yes, plural of Spanish word for sorrow, pain" adding, "but your last name offers redemption, a second chance, if you will. Lazarus rising from death."

"Or a leprous beggar."

"I prefer my New Testament parable to yours."

"As you will, sorry to interrupt," she gestured for him to continue.

"So, all in all, a name with a sense of both past and future. A full life, one way or the other."

"I feel as if my fortune's just been told."

"It's a high hand, but not a straight."

"Well, mister cosmic philosopher," she rested a hand on his back, as she slid off the bar stool. "Perhaps our paths will cross again at the foothills of the moon. Right now, however, I'm due to dine at the captain's table." She took a step or two before turning around again: "What do I call you, by the way?"

"Cosmic Charlie is fine," he said, signing the tab: C.O. Jones.

COJONES

After a surfeit of surf and turf, guests of the Fiesta FunShip separated post-meal according to age group. Younger kids trundled off to be tucked in for the night. Adolescents feigned retirement, only to sneak out later. Adults beelined for Vegas-style entertainment in the ship's main nightclub, among them one C.O. Jones, who sailed smoothly towards a table a few feet from the performers. The cabaret act on stage seemed to be working the kinks out of an uninspired and poorly coordinated review. The crowd didn't seem to mind and grew rowdier with each passing flash of thigh.

LEGS, LEGS, LEGS!" yelled a man, who jumped up and down excitedly, offering a gesture somewhere between an air high-five and Nixon's V sign for victory. His unabashed enthusiasm went on for some time before a visibly furious wife took a firm grip on the waistband of his sansibelt slacks and jerked him back into his seat.

C.O. Jones focused his attention away from this pitiable scene. Even through the glare of the klieg lights, his glance fell almost immediately upon his companion of earlier that afternoon. He sent the waiter over with a note inviting her to share his table.

"I'm pleased you could join me," he held the chair as she smoothed the folds of her evening dress. The rich chocolate colored fabric accentuated her delicate form and brought warmth to her dark hair and eyes. She looked lovely and he told her so. She was gracious in accepting the compliment, remarking that he, in dinner jacket, cleaned up rather nicely too.

"My turn to do the honors. What's your poison? Is there an appropriate concoction for viewing such…" she motioned towards the stage, "gam gazing?"

"I understand the can-can troop trots off after this number. It's to be followed by gentler fare, so I'd recommend we skip the champagne and settle down with brandy."

He flagged down a server. "Armagnac, please."

"Right away, Mr. Jones."

"Charlie Jones is it?" she asked.

"C.O., actually, but go ahead and call me 'Charlie.' It bonds us."

She opened her mouth to reply, but her words were drowned out by a loud drum roll announcing the next act. A grand piano descended from the ceiling. Upon it, a honey-haired beauty with light almond eyes and a smile that could melt butter. It might have been the spray of heather pinned to her breast or the faint trace of freckles across the bridge of her nose, but something set her apart from the typical songstress. She conveyed an impish innocence, which seemed to disarm even this audience. The bayed crowd waited patiently to hear her sing. When she did, they swooned. Soaring through many octaves, her voice shone clear, full, and powerful. The old familiar words reverberated with fresh appeal.

Frank observed these phenomena with fascination. Even his guest appeared entranced. Curious, he picked up the plastic stand and read the nightly entertainment place card encased within. He quoted aloud: "Looking at her is like sucking on butterscotch."

"Strangely, so true, even if prosaic," his companion responded vaguely, her attention still focused on stage.

As Frank returned his gaze to the torch singer, the lighting changed from blue to a soft tea-rose tone, as she began a slow slide off her piano. And then, she walked amongst them, a tall tawny form in shimmering silk, trailing chords.

> *You do something to me, something*
> *that simply mystifies me, tell me,*
> *why should it be*
> *You've got the power to hypnotize me…*

As she circled the tables towards the back, gasps of delight rose with laughter and applause.

"Charlie, can you see what's going on?"

"Not really. Is she holding something up? I'm not sure. It looks like a watch." He turned back to his companion, "I suppose we'll see it for ourselves soon enough."

> *Let me live 'neath your spell.*
> *Let you do that voodoo that you do so well...*

By now it had become clear that the minx was mixing prestidigitation in with her vocal act. She'd lift lipsticks, cameras, kerchiefs, and room keys off of unsuspecting audience members, incorporating the items into the lyrics then handing them off to the victim's table mates. She was reaching the soaring heights of the ballad's final notes as she passed those closest to the stage. The crowd roared to a standing ovation as she finished. "Brava, brava!" they called. She took a low curtsy and whispered into the microphone: "My, aren't you sweet."

More thunderous applause followed, until she settled the crowd with a hand. "Now I have a story to tell. Do you want to hear my story?" Whoops of assent followed. "I have a big heart, you know, but it only belongs to one person. Who out there know who my heart belongs to?" she stirred.

"To Daddy!" the fans yelled.

"Well, that was before. There's someone very new in my life now..." the chanteuse purred, holding up a wallet she'd concealed in the folds of her gown. Opening it, she began an Ella-style scat refrain:

> *my-ba-dee-da doo-ya*
> *a-heart-eo la-la*
> *Be-bop be-bop longs-ah*
> *My heart-be-be-longs-to-ooo-lo-la*
> *To-you-deo-you you*
> *Frankie-eo Frankie o-beboppin-baby*
> *Do-ya-do-ya-be-bop*
> *My. Heart. Be. Longs. tooooo Frankieeeeee.*

The crowd loved the lark and looked around to find the fellow audience member lucky enough to have his driver's license lifted and celebrated in such a fashion. After the devilish diva tossed the pilfered billfold back to its owner and left the stage, he was forgotten, by all but one: his table mate, who'd found this public unveiling very enlightening indeed. Exposed, yet quiescent, the hapless man cleared his throat and leaned forward over the dying applause. "How about a stroll?"

"With whom?"

"Frank Wayne."

"Lead on, Frankie," said the woman known as Dolores Lazar.

MOONDANCE

Frank offered his curious companion a limited explanation for his presence on board the cruise ship under an assumed name. He said that he had something of a personal grudge against the company founder, Miguel Santos, but suggested that the trip was an impetuous lark and his mission harmless. He did not admit to the involvement of other individuals and made no mention of recent history like the CALB debacle in Miami. He did confess that he'd guessed her true identity early on, describing himself as a devotee of Washington's social pages, in which journalists, especially attractive ones, would frequently be featured.

Brooke wasn't sure what she was dealing with, but Frank seemed worth some tentative trust. So, she admitted that Dolores Lazar was a fake name; yet withheld any hint of what she was currently working on or why it necessitated a false name.

There they were, at the railings, Frank Wayne and Brooke Glaze, sketching cautious circles around each other. Both were keenly aware of the unspoken secrets to be earned, traded, tricked, and possibly shared out of mutual necessity in the days ahead. They'd get no further tonight. Taking the next step would require time apart to reassess. Their mutual reserve validated this understanding. The night's splendor shimmered before them. In every direction, the moon's changeable face rippled before slipping into darkness.

MORNING DUE

Peter and Ada had been waiting for Ben O. Davey to return. The Congressman's beeper had gone off just as his young cohorts were concluding their report on Frank's coded message and the eavesdropped audio-taped conversation. Ada spooned the last syrupy strawberry from her plate and made an offering. Peter accepted it readily and began to speak. He was interrupted, however, by Ben's return.

Ben seemed distracted, but Ada wondered if Ben had caught this sign of intimacy.

"Sorry to be so long." He reclaimed his seat and looked around impatiently. "I had to use the phone in the manager's private suite. It's four flights up!" Ben exhaled indulgently before coming finally to the choice news: "My office was holding Frank on the line. He was in a public booth somewhere on the island of St. Maarten. I guess the cruise ship made port there. Anyhow, they patched him through, so I was able to let him know you'd solved his riddle and found a cassette tape in the post box. He wouldn't tell me who he got to bug Brooke Glaze's phone, but he did say this was the first recording. It hadn't arrived at the P.O. Box before he left. It was quite a surprise when he realized that she was on board."

"Actually, on the same ship?" asked Ada in disbelief.

Ben nodded. "And they've met, talked in fact, although neither has given the other much explanation as to what they're after."

"The tape fills in a lot. On her side, at least. We've now

confirmed there's a snitch stoking Brooke Glaze's fires. We know the informant's identity remains a mystery, even to Brooke herself. And we know her travel arrangements were made by this secretive source."

Peter tapped his chin thoughtfully. "Why a cruise?" Turning to Ben, "Did you ask him what made him get on the boat in the first place?"

"Following Willie Sutton's advice, I suspect."

"To go where the money is?"

"Right. Speaking of banks, the cruise business seems to be the Bat's major source of cash."

"Did you tell him about the classified reports and the Cabal's press release?"

Ben savored the final pulpy dregs of his orange juice before nodding. "A condensed briefing only...he had to ring off. The ship will be back out at sea by now, I expect. We'll just have to wait, and see what, if anything, he discovers next."

"In the very least, he's got a stronger hand to bluff with where Brooke Glaze is concerned. Maybe he can get her to ante up more on this anonymous caller."

"Perhaps I'll make another trip to the Intel Committee. A quick survey of the latest Caribbean traffic might be informative," Ben mused. The sound of his beeper brought him out of this reverie and up onto his feet. "Duty calls," he glanced back and forth between them, "you two keep doing what you've been doing. You make a good team. Yes, very good. Gotta run."

Ben was off before noticing the flush of crimson he'd left behind.

ACES

Befitting the nature of their second colloquy, Brooke and Frank agreed to meet in the ship's casino. Unwilling to give away any clues ahead of the real match of wits, they opted to skip the tables altogether and head straight for the bar. They traded small talk for a few moments, then cut to the chase.

Frank's loaded deck allowed him to gain an early upper hand. Brooke admitted that a tipster had been promising revelations about Santos – no hard leads or even a hint about the nature of the scandal, as yet. Her instincts told her to stick with it. That was the only reason she'd risked a run-around on the high seas and agreed to the silly alias. Brooke also claimed to have no clue about the source's identity, though she believed it to be someone with direct access to the Bat's inner circle.

Frank didn't press and Brook made the most of her information deficit. She unilaterally disarmed, confirming to Frank what he'd hinted he already knew, then made a pitch for reciprocal privileges. She argued that their best chance of gleaning any kind of insight from this misadventure was to start digging, an activity executed more safely and efficiently in partnership. Frank concurred. They agreed to join forces.

Having formed a team, they began to plot. A cocktail napkin was employed to lay out the disparate threads. They hoped that, thus rendered, the various strings might suggest connections and reveal traces of a larger pattern. Wishful thinking. Needless to say, a neat tapestry failed to emerge. Nonetheless, subtle shades of significance stood out. What did quietly revised broadcast frequencies, unreported defections, and a reporter being sent on an unsolicited cruise holiday have to connect them? Comings and goings? Brooke must have been sent on this cruise for a reason. The ship itself seemed as good a place as any to search for answers. But where to begin? And what to look for?

The duo settled on a two-pronged strategy. They would monitor any unusual occurrences or behavior on board; and identify restricted areas of the vessel and hunt for evidence of anything untoward. Perimeter surveillance was just a matter of taking turns on night watch. The task of searching the ship's vast, labyrinthine interior promised to be daunting and time-consuming. What they really needed was to get hold of a blueprint or chatty crew member for intimate knowledge of the layout. Frank and Brooke sat mulling this to the rattle of roulette balls, the scroll of one-armed bandits, and the shuffle of fortune's marked cards. Then, it seems, lady luck herself paid them a visit.

"Pardon the interruption. You left so quickly last night that I hadn't a chance to thank you for being such good sports," she continued: "I hope you didn't mind my little routine. I worried that I might have upset you."

"My dear, please, it was a pleasure," Frank beamed, swiveling his stool toward the singer, "My heart will always be yours to claim, as will my wallet." Gesturing to his left, "would you care to join us?"

"Thank you. Let me buy this next round in appreciation."

Frank and Brooke exchanged a glance, and both nodded. The golden-throated beauty with the fetching smile looked much younger without the stage lights and slinky gown. The scampish streak evident in subtle hues the previous evening showed through more clearly absent any makeup. She hopped into the seat and whistled for the barman. "Potions, please," she commanded sweetly.

"Comin' up, May," the man responded with gusto.

"I'm May. I know you're Franklin Aristotle Wayne – I never forget a name." Turning towards Brooke, she put out her hand.

"Brooke Glaze"

"You have beautiful eyes, Ms. Glaze, I noticed them last night."

"Oh," Brooke broke into an unguarded grin, "well, thanks and please, call me Brooke."

The drinks arrived. "To May and her magical musical ways," Frank cheered. After they'd all had a sip, Frank continued: "But where, if I can ask, did you learn your witchcraft?"

"The sticky fingers?" she giggled, "it's actually rather a blue tale." May peered through her long lashes, "bawdy, I mean."

"Do tell," Brooke challenged.

May's face lit up at the prospect of spinning a yarn. She propped her elbows up on the bar, drawing them to her with a confiding air. "It's humorous, in a perverse way," she began. "I'm not supposed to talk about it…certainly not with guests!" Obviously disinclined to heed official rules, she went on, "Most of the staff knows, but they're all so serious."

Laying a hand across his heart, Frank vowed cheerfully: "We promised not to report you.

After another sip to whet the words, May's tale began.

"The lounge act is new. Just two weeks so far. It's what I've always wanted to do. Well, singing for an audience, at least. Anyhow, the FunShip wasn't actually looking for a cabaret act when I first applied for work. Their big star was an illusionist, Magnus Manticore. He was a huge draw. People love to suspend disbelief, especially when on vacation." She sighed reflectively. "Magnus performed all the usual stunts: saw a woman in two, escape from a locked cage, you know. It was standard fare, but always dramatic. Anyhow, Magnus needed an able-bodied assistant and I fit the bill. Actually, I think it was more that I fit the costume, such as it was. It worked out well, for a time. My fingers were nimble, and Magnus helped me polish my technique." She paused briefly to jiggle the ice cubes loose from the side of her glass. Shaking her head at the memory: "We used to do this one routine – a mind-reading gag with a twist. Instead of asking an audience member to hand me an item to be identified by the blindfolded magician, I'd instead lift something off of them. They'd be so stunned by my ability to pick pockets that they'd forget to consider this might be an easy set up for Magnus's guessing game."

"Obfuscation is a weapon."

May continued, "Magnus was a decent illusionist, but he was a very *indecent* human being. He drank like a fish and could behave like a beast – always groping and slurring: 'howz about some pocus- pocus, honey. Wanna pull my rabbit ears.' Well, you get the picture."

Frank and Brooke both grimaced at the image.

Speaking lightly, May went on: "I think I was the first assistant that stood up to him, rather than quitting or complying. It drove him mad. The binges got worse and worse. He lost interest in the act and basically stopped showing up. I had to start carrying things solo. After he got fired, but before the ship returned to port, he'd spend all night in the casino bar, going table to table doing clown tricks. For a few evenings the patrons thought it was fun and management tolerated it, but he pushed things too far."

"Go on," Brooke urged.

"He'd been twisting animals out of balloons; poodles, giraffes, etc. He started to make dozens of them, handing them out to all the kids. The trouble started when some parents looked a little more closely. Not only were the animals endowed with graphic anatomical details, but their not-so-private parts had been magnified to startling proportions."

Frank and Brooke stared at May, then looked at each other and burst into laughter.

"Can you imagine all the devout church-goers that we get on board having to explain to their children what had happened to the poor animals."

"Well, art is meant to be provocative!"

May wrapped up her story, after signaling the barman for a second round. "The FunShip needed a more permanent replacement act. I wasn't good enough to lean on just the magic alone, so they let me sing, provided I mix in a little of the old trickery."

As the fresh drinks arrived, Frank cast a conspiratorial eye on Brooke, whose mouth curved slyly in assent.

"May, dear," Frank began.

"Mr. Wayne?"

"Frank, please," he continued, "Brooke and I have a story of our own to tell. Would you be free to take an early dinner with us before the show?"

"Can I make a confession?" she asked, looking from one to the other.

Frank and Brooke both nodded.

"I'm lucky to have swung this gig, but honestly, I'm bored out of my skull. There was something about the two of you that seemed exciting. Like there might be some mischief in the air. I added that scat routine and picked Frank's pocket, hoping for an excuse to meet you."

"If it's an adventure you're looking for, we're the ones in luck," Brooke winked.

Let's avoid the main dining areas," Frank added.

May's eyes were sparkling, "How about the piano bar at six?"

At the appointed hour, the three met and a plan was hatched.

HOCUS POCUS

May cast a winning smile over her left shoulder. "That's right, just match my moves." Her arms mapped a new wave hand jive. Her hips swung to the funky beat. She sang along to the sound of the boom box.

Her partner kept up as best he could. Rico Pérez was neither tall, nor dark, nor handsome. This isn't to say that he wasn't visually affecting. He was. Epic weight room sessions and a full catalogue of steroid enhancers gave him the appearance of an inverted triangle: a polygon with an obscenely broad base, whittling abruptly to a pair of tassel-tied loafers. The too-small head above his massive shoulders sported a Marine-style buzz cut bleached Billy Idol blond. His shiny eyes, which were tinted by colored contact lenses, looked about as focused as marbles.

The duo made quite a sight. Chased by a tight tempo, they rode the rhythm. May worked it. Rico followed her lead like a puppy.

Giddy with pride and stunned by his good fortune, Rico tried to center his attention on achieving something approximating physical grace. To have been chosen by such a goddess as her practice partner on a new dance step seemed a sign of great spiritual significance to young Rico. I'm in heaven, he kept thinking to himself."

And then it was over. *Llorado se fue!* She pulled out of his embrace quickly. So quickly, in fact, that he didn't notice she'd lifted the keys from his pocket. Rico, night security officer for Santos Cruise Lines, would have been in seventh heaven to know how close her skilled fingers had come to his manhood, as she deftly removed the master set. As it was, he remained innocent of their disappearance. The keys would be returned unscathed, but not unused, before he could register their loss.

HOT POTATO

Frank won muted applause from a group of contemporaries waiting for their wives to return from the day's jaunt into port, not for anything he himself brought back on board, but for the two beautiful younger women who greeted him on deck.

"I fear your loveliness makes us conspicuous," he murmured, as May and Brooke bracketed him.

"Slip me the duplicates. I'm meeting Rico in 45 minutes," May said, holding her hand near his.

Frank tried a paternal look, "No more *Lambada* or whatever, right? We've asked you to take enough risks already."

May wrinkled her nose, animating her deceptively delicate features. "I promise, no more forbidden dances." Marking a cross over his heart, she winked farewell.

"Aren't you forgetting something?" Frank prompted, reaching for the master keys.

She took a step back towards him, whispering: "I already took the liberty."

Frank pulled out an empty pocket. "Picked clean."

"Glad she's on our side," Brooke chuckled, as they both watched May float up the stairwell.

FIRE DRILL

A chance passerby might think romance drove the couple to huddle close by the lower deck railing. Brooke and Frank, of course, had other motives for being awake and together at 3:15 am.

They were there to keep a lookout for anything astir in the cool ink of night. Thus far, the far-off lights of Santo Domingo were the only signs of life. Frank used hushed tones to describe his day in port, hunting for a discreet locksmith to match the keys May had lifted from Rico. They both marveled at what an asset May was proving. She had ascertained the existence of an unused storage area in the ship's hull by asking Rico about places for couples to be "alone" on board. After sending Rico away for a glass of water, she'd peeked at the daily rosters and found notations for pre-dawn arrival times. Of what and from where, however, there was no indication. These discoveries did seem to explain why the ship needed a night watchman. It also explained why the company had hired someone as dim as Rico. Best not to have anyone too sharp and inquisitive managing secret off-hours arrivals.

Based on this new knowledge, May was now somewhere within that secret storage room, while Frank and Brooke kept sentry.

"What's that?"

Frank turned his ear towards the water.

"Motor," he said after a few seconds of listening. "Definitely an out-board motor." He crouched behind the life vest locker to his left and drew Brooke down with him: "No need to call attention to ourselves."

Brooke widened her dark eyes, as the small craft pulled alongside the cruise ship. Their view was obscured, but still clear enough to reveal the movement of boxes from one vessel to the other. In less than 20 minutes, the visiting boat had been emptied of its contents. Yet it still lingered, bobbing against the host ship's massive hull. Brooke stole a questioning look at her companion, who shrugged, similarly confused.

"Why hang around?" Brooke finally asked.

"Wish I knew," Frank breathed quietly.

"I'm worried about May."

Frank nodded. "Look," he nudged. Shadowy figures appeared. They began to reload the smaller craft with the same number of boxes that they'd offloaded earlier. Then the boat pulled away and disappeared behind the black curtain of the sea.

"Does that mean something went wrong? Were those the same boxes being brought back or new ones?"

"Let's just get out of here," Frank took her hand, "We need a diversion. There's no sign of May."

"Fire alarm?"

Frank nodded approvingly. "The high school fail-safe." He rose and found one of the iconic red boxes a few yards down the passageway. He used the chained hammer to shatter the glass and pulled down the activation lever.

The noise was deafening. It shook the ship awake. Passengers began streaming into the open in various stages of consciousness and dress. Frank and Brooke trained their eyes across the swelling crowd, in search of their friend.

FunShip staff were beginning to take control, imploring folks to remain calm and stationary, insisting that no signs of fire or smoke had been detected. Just a false alarm, they counseled reassuringly. Through the chaos of curlers and PJs, they spotted May.

When certain that she'd caught their attention, May began to walk. They followed at a safe distance. May passed Frank's room, turning briefly to glance at them as she did so. They took the hint and went inside, leaving the door ajar. She joined minutes later.

SHOW AND TELL

"Have a sip. You've had a scare."

May touched Frank's elbow before taking the glass. "I could say the same for you two."

Brooke tried to lighten things with a toast, passing around three cups of whiskey: "To being in the same boat."

May smiled and took a gulp. "The fire alarm was your doing, yes? It helped. I don't think I was detected, by the way."

"What happened in the storage hold?" Brooke asked.

"The key worked like a charm," May began. "All seemed quiet, so I went in for a closer look. The only light was a glow from an illuminated emergency exit sign, but I could make out about three or four dozen crates stacked up. They basically filled the room. I had crouched down to try reading the markings, when I heard a voice. It was Rico, telling someone in Spanish that he'd be back to lock up in a half-hour." May paused to wet her lips with more single malt. "I figured that would give me enough time to introduce myself to God and confess my sins, before being thrown to the sharks!" May laughed into another sip. "Sorry, wound a bit tightly now…Okay, so I slipped behind one of the crates at the far end. Thankfully, the two guys who entered the room didn't turn on any lights. The bad news came when they began removing the crates that formed my hiding place."

"Oh, May!" Brooke shook her head.

"But you won't believe this. Just as I was beginning to really freak out, one of them started bringing crates back into the room.

Out went one crate; in came another. I guess initially they needed the extra space to make the exchanges, but once half the room was empty, they could alternate trips. I slipped over to hide behind some of the new crates, to see if the marking were any different. As I moved along the rear wall, I came across one of the original crates, which had cracked open, so I dug my hand past the packing materials and took a sample."

Frank and Brooke just stared, as May pulled up her sweatshirt to reveal a brown wooden box tucked into her waist band.

"They're supposed to be quite good," she said nonchalantly, handing them her prize.

"Sweet flights of fancy," Frank exclaimed, "they're *Cohibas* from the Dominican Republic.

"Cigars?"

"Yes, my dear Ms. Glaze, cigars. The true *Cohibas* are made in Havana, but the D.R. began rolling their own branded version to capitalize on the embargo restrictions. Since the Cuban ones are contraband in America, the Dominican variety became the best available alternative." Frank drummed his index finger on the table in front of him, "there's something else," he began to say.

Brooke turned to May: "What about the other crates, did you get a look?"

"Only from the outside. The rest were still sealed and intact. There was a distinction though. They bore the same insignia on the seal, but the lettering on the old ones was in Spanish, but in English on the new ones."

Frank raised an eyebrow. "Was it a full switch?"

"Seemed to be one for one. They'd just finished when the fire bell went off. Thankfully, this was before Rico had returned to lock up, so I took my cue and split."

"You're brave." Brooke put a hand on May's shoulder.
May took Brooke's hand in her own. They watched Frank begin to open the wooden box.

He extracted one of the purloined *puros*, holding it between his index and middle finger. "Might as well," he proclaimed.

"You first," Brooke said.

"Yes, after you," said May.

"Delighted to play guinea pig," Frank patted his pockets in increasing frustration, muttering: "Where is my blasted guillotine?" As their laughter grew, so did Frank's suspicion. When he looked up, he saw his cigar clipper resting in May's palm.

"How on earth did you just do that?" Frank exclaimed.

"I'm not that good! I've had it since I lifted your wallet and brought it with me to hand it back."

Frank smiled, as he clipped the end and lit a match. He inhaled with passionate care and exhaled with considerably less enjoyment. A frown formed, as Frank held the cigar in front of him for a better view. "Humph." With one end still lit, he split the cigar down the center, turning what he found inside out towards the others.

"Is that...?" Brooke began.

"Why is it green," May interjected. "Aren't the leaves supposed to be brown?"

Frank smirked, "richer than you'd ever know from sniffing them!" Using the clipper's sharp point, he slit the unlit side of the *Cohiba* down the full length, peeling off the outer tobacco covering to reveal a tightly rolled stack of American C-notes.

"Hundred-dollar bills!" May exclaimed.

"Mint condition," Frank added.

Brooke took one from the pile still curled in Frank's hand. "Mint is right. These are the new issue, the redesigned, bigger, balder, more counterfeit-proof Ben Franklins that Treasury just issued."

Chapter 9

LIBERTY & JUSTICE

My homeland is Cuba and the night. We are islands exiled from the light of freedom. Pawns in a larger game, we operate in darkness. We have our ways. Soy como un golpe de estado.

100 TOO

luminous tendril of celestial wish
...the keen illimitable secret of begin

"Penny for your thoughts, Peter?"

"Are they worth so little," he grinned.

Ada dug into her jacket and brought out a shiny nickel. "Much more and I'm willing to pay," she tossed the bounty in the air.

Peter caught it and pressed the coin to her forehead. "Open sesame," he commanded.

Ada poked his midsection: "You first."

"Fair enough. I was thinking about the bulls of Pamplona. Do you know when the festival of San Fermin begins?"

"Early July, right? But seriously…"

"I am being serious." He took her hand. "Come on."

"Are we off to see the bulls?" Ada goaded, matching his lanky stride.

They had been walking back to the Hill from their breakfast meeting with Ben. The couple had just passed the point where Pennsylvania Avenue runs into Constitution and the grounds of the Capitol begin, when Peter detoured them towards a bench in a secluded section of the Senate gardens.

Peter took a thin book of e.e. cummings *100 Select Poems* from his back pocket. "Pick one."

Ada sat down beside him, as she flipped through the pages. "What's the rule on carnal pleasure in federal shrubbery?" she asked.

"Mandatory sentencing."

"We should lobby for reform."

"We should, but not right now. In fact, I don't even want to talk about our jaunt to Spain."

Their touches grew more reckless, until a small voice interrupted their embrace. James Janssen, Jr. the most precocious 6th grader in Mrs. Young's civics class at Fairfield Academy in Summit, New Jersey. Jimmy had broken away from the pack on their way to meet their State's senior Senator. Imagine his delight, in finding the embarrassed couple amidst the greenery.

When confident that his classmates were within range, the class clown called out: "Is this a petting zoo, or what?"

Ada and Peter laughed. She picked up the poetry collection again, pretending to read, and Jimmy Jr. returned to the applause of his admiring peers.

SIXES + SEVENS

The Citizens for Open Government office was already bustling when Director Vane and his research assistant arrived at half-past nine in the morning. Some skilled bobbing and weaving got them through the busy reception area to the stairwell. One short flight up landed them in Peter's office. Rosie gave a casual salute from the vicinity of the printer, before plunging her hands back into said machine's obscure interior.

Peter winced at the memory of his secretary's previous repair endeavors. Tentatively, Peter approached the yawning jaws of the printer to peer inside. Rods and rotors, spools and sliders, inky cartridges, and other formerly functional elements glared back from the depths. Rosie elbowed him back and dove in again like a mad scientist bent on revelation.

"Shouldn't you be trained to…ah…operate like that, Rosie?" Peter joked.

"Or have some form of signed consent." Ada added.

"As if each of you alone weren't enough to drive me crazy?! Now you're working tag team on teasing me," Rosie protested, trying hard not to smile. "Where have you two been anyway? I've got pictures from Gene's school pageant to show you."

Rosie looked for a tissue to wipe her hands and caught Peter and Ada exchanging a private look. "oh my," Rosie pursed her lips with a satisfied air.

She pointed at a phone pad, "Messages for the pair of you this morning."

THE ELEVEN

Peter approached the desk with a tinge of guilt not uncommon in workaholics testing alternative treatments. Being raised essentially without parents had given him a drive to make a difference with his one lone life. He knew his mother and father as people of mission, but not as caregivers. Frank had shown him warmth and friendship, instilling in him his first real awareness of affection and its power to feed the soul. Peter desired both success and happiness. Thus far, he'd figured these goals could be reached on a linear path – one first and then the other. Maybe, he'd been wrong. Could they align along the way? These new ponderings were confusing. Simple tasks, he thought, lets stick to those for now. Smiling to himself, he swiveled into his chair and wheeled up to his desk.

Peter opened mail, pushed papers left to right, penned a memo, flipped through his weekly planner, ranked to-dos by urgency, and then reached for the phone. As he picked it up, he had one of those flashes. He had let Ada in; and it felt good.

He looked up. Her head was down, focused on a piece of paper pinched between the thumb and pointer fingers.

Peter restrained himself from disturbing her. He just watched for a few seconds longer, then began to dial.

"Hey," she said, moving towards him, still staring at the note in her hands.

Peter replaced the receiver.

"Oh, sorry, go ahead," she said.

"It can wait," he replied, "what's up?"

"My friend Jaime, Peralta's aide. This message says he rang and wants me to call back as soon as possible."

Peter nodded. "What are you waiting for?"

"I haven't heard from him since Miami. I sort of figured that it might be the end of the friendship."

"Well, he's obviously got something on his mind." Peter stood up. "I'm going to see if I can help Rosie with that copier. Use the phone in privacy. This may take a while!"

"Thanks, Peter."

"Good luck."

CRAZY 8

An officious voice answered: "Office of Congressman Peralta."

"Jaime Acosta, please."

"May I tell him who is calling?"

"Ada Tremont."

"And you are with?'

"I'm returning his call. He knows me."

"Please hold."

After a brief pause. "Ada? Hi, how are you?"

"Fine. Good. You?"

"Well, I guess you got my message. Yeah, of course you did, that's why you're calling." He was speaking quickly.

"Jaime. I'm glad to hear from you," she offered. "Whether it's just to clear the air or if there's something more, I want you to know…"

"Ada," he cut in, "I…well, thanks for saying that. I need your help. Something's come up."

"Name it."

"Can we get together?"

"Of course.

"I'd like to meet right away." She could tell that he was cupping the phone, talking in a whisper.

"Okay. Where?"

"Garden behind the Shakespeare museum. On South Capitol."

INFINITY ON ITS SIDE

"What's with the cloak and dagger? Afraid I'll ruin your reputation?" Ada joked, trying to force a crack in Jaime's unnaturally stern expression.

"Ada. I can't even tell you how good it feels just to see you." He sat down heavily beside her, rubbing his eyes. "You'll think I'm crazy. I didn't know who else to turn to, who wouldn't think I was nuts."

"Jaime. Please, just tell me what's going on. It's hard to shock me these days," she said with a nudge.

Staring forward towards the garden's entrance, his voice took on a business-like tone. "I'm going to leave in a minute." Ada made a noise of protest, but he silenced her with a quick imploring look. "Please, just listen," he continued. "The bag I'm sliding between us will stay behind. When you return to your office and open it, you'll see it's a roll of $100 bills. If you look carefully, you may be able to tell they are fakes. They are copies of the newly designed C-notes; and they are excellent copies. What you need to know is that I found them wrapped inside a cigar. The wrapping is in the bag too. I don't know who sent it. It fell out amongst some travel brochures that were sent to my office."

"Travel brochures?"

Jaime took a deep breath and turned his head towards his friend. "FunShip Cruises. The Santos Lines." He rose abruptly. "Call me at home tonight," he stood abruptly and left.

Ada waited for him to disappear from sight, and then she counted to eighty-eight. Her lucky number and a decent interval. Slipping the bag under her arm, she looked around. She seemed to be alone among the flaming Sugar Maples.

DOUBLE TAKE

Rosie knocked before entering. "Can I bring you some lunch? It's nearing 3 p.m."

"Already?" Ada looked up vaguely. "Oh, no thanks," more focused, "I'll pick up a bite on the way. I have an errand to run. If Peter gets back or calls in…"

"I'll tell him you've been itching to speak with him."

Pecking Rosie on the cheek on her way, Ada confided, "Back in an hour."

"Don't forget to eat, sugar."

Ada vanished around the corner, down the stairs, and out onto the street. Autumn's weather was crisp and fair. Hill denizens bustled about Eastern Market, clutching coffee cups, to-go lunches, bags of orchard-fresh apples, and even the occasional bunch of flowers, to take back to their offices. Rosie's motherly prompting echoed in Ada's head, she ducked into Roaster's for a cup of joe and a bagel for the road.

Munching and sipping, she crossed the street to the Metro. "Arg, did I forget the key?" Ada mumbled to herself. A quick check in her bag, "Phew." She slugged more java and descended the stairs.

I'm getting better she decided. Even though my friend just handed me a wad of fake cash, I'm remaining calm. Even though Peter isn't around, I'm not pacing nervously waiting for direction. I'm going to be chill and constructive. I promised Quinn that I'd swing by his place to check on mail, plants, and such. That'll keep my mind off this funny money.

Ada resumed her internal dialogue after boarding the train bound for Chinatown. Quinn. Peter. Life had become complicated.

SILHOUETTE

The sky was yellow and the sun was blue

Every few days, Peter would head to a basketball court not far from work for a pick-up game. He'd grown tight with a few of the regulars, who would gather at Tunicliff's Tavern for a quick jar or to catch a little NBA action on the TV above the bar. He was happy to see these familiar faces as he entered the yard. Lex, a tall twenty-something, with a mean reverse lay-up and a wicked hip-check, waved.

"Wassup, PV. Early today, old man. Lose that suit and jump in."

Having greeted Peter and distracted his opposition, Lex faked left, dusted his defender, and drove hard to the basket.

"You ready for a piece of that, PV?" he taunted.

"Actually," Peter called back, "I need a favor."

Lex curled his long arm in a hailing motion and four other players jogged off the court. Their opposition looked relieved.

"What's it?"

Peter began: "I need numbers. You all willing to take a trip to Chinatown with me?" Adding, "I don't know what we're walking into."

"PV," Lex intoned to a chorus of snickering, "know how funny you sound? Let's blaze!"

That settled, Peter and the squad piled into two cabs and headed northwest to 7th and H.

The taxi that Peter rode in arrived first. He directed the driver to slow down and pull up just beyond the building, out of view. The second cabbie followed. The six of them looked up at stone and scaffolding. Peter was hoping the next step would occur to him."

"Renovated flats," Billy D, the group's finesse player, stated authoritatively.

"How's that?" asked Peter.

"You know. Artsy types. Gentrification. My uncle runs a construction company. He's "in" with the Mayor. I worked for him last summer," pointing up, "on that."

Turns out Billy had rigged the electrical boxes on the building in question. The building Quinn had just vacated. They began to set a game plan in motion.

BLIND SIGHTED

"If you told me what you were looking for, maybe I could help," Ada ventured, in as convincing a tone as she could muster. She was tied to a kitchen chair, watching her captor paw clumsily through Quinn's belongings. Her initial terror had subsided. In fact, the man seemed more nervous than she. He was visibly distracted, almost at a loss as to how to proceed with a prisoner as audience. It didn't take police training to recognize that his was no carefully calibrated robbery routine. Whatever search skills he may have arrived with, Ada's unexpected appearance had robbed him of both coordination and composure. His jittery behavior would have worried her more had he a weapon. As it was, he seemed to be unarmed and showed no signs of getting physical.

There was an odd look to his eyes. Furtive. Fanatical. Druidic. Also, familiar. Maybe from a movie? Ada was trying to remember. Could it be? Then it hit her. Was this the man from her first visit to Peter's house; the guy who had run into her; whose hat she'd knocked off; who'd peered at her with the same freaky gaze? He seemed to become aware of her again, quitting his haphazard hunting and fixing her with rattled intensity. He knelt down before the chair to which she was bound. He too seemed to have made the connection. "You!" he said, "Who sent you here?"

"I'm here to get the mail for my friend. I don't understand any of this." And she didn't. She couldn't see any reason why a weirdo who loitered around Peter's neighborhood would be ransacking Quinn's apartment.

The stranger lisped his consonant combinations in accented English, giving his speech an unnatural hissing quality. "Lady, you lie to me," he narrowed his eyes, "you are working with Mr. Peter Vane. I know this!"

"He's my boss. But Quinn is my friend. From school. Not work. I came for Quinn. For the mail."

He glared at her and placed a kitchen rag in her mouth. "I will not remove this," he tugged on the gag, "unless you do as I say."

Ada nodded her consent.

"You are to call Mr. Peter Vane. You will instruct him to bring all evidence he has to you. Here. Give him the address and make him come. He must bring everything. No tricks. I will be listening to all that you say."

Ada wondered what the hell kind of evidence he wanted Peter to bring. Could he possibly know about the bag from Jaime? Or the tape recording of the call to Brooke Glaze? No way, she decided. The man hadn't been following her, hadn't even recognized her at first, so he couldn't know about the counterfeit notes or the tape. The man was yelling at her. She shook her head to remind him she was still gagged.

"*Apúrate*! Call!" he barked, banging the phone down in front of her.

He freed her mouth and held the receiver an inch from her ear, as she told him the number to dial. Peter knows me, Ada thought to herself. I can tip him off without this goon realizing. I just need to be careful.

Rosie must have been away from her desk. Peter picked right up.

"Mr. Vane, sir. It's Ada Tremont, from the intern pool."

That was twenty minutes ago. Now, she sat waiting, hoping that help was on the way. Her captor stalked back and forth along the bank of windows, peering out from time to time, but mostly engrossed in internal argument. He would seem to forget about her, then look over suspiciously. She's behaving, his self-satisfied look said. He imagined that he might be rewarded for delivering an even bigger prize that than the one he'd been sent to find.

"Coño!" he cursed, as several large explosions echoed through the apartment structure. The unmistakable stench of short-circuited fuses and burning wires followed. The stranger looked at Ada with wild eyes. She projected a look of alarm and fear to disguise the excitement she felt. He lunged at her taking the gag from her mouth again. "We have to get out of here," she panted, "it smells electrical. We'll be burned alive. You must untie me," she commanded.

The man, accustomed to orders grew more confused: "Quiet! I must think," he covered his ears, gripping his head.

"No time. We must escape. Do it, untie me!" Ada demanded.

The role reversal worked. He rushed to loosen her ties, enough for her to slip out. "I go first. Do not follow me. Stay away," his voice became desperate. "Stay away," he pled again as he climbed onto the fire escape and began descending.

Ada twisted free, thinking that this damn well better be the diversion she'd been counting on and not a real emergency. She had just stood up when Peter and his squad stormed in.

"He had me hostage," she called out, pointing to the fire escape.

Peter rushed towards her. "You okay?"

"I think so."

One of the others, Lex, broke the moment. "You want us to chase him, PV?"

Peter shook his head. "We're here to rescue, not capture."

"Thank you so much!" Ada called out as Lex and his buddies turned to go.

"Any time pretty lady. Check you later, PV."

When they'd left, Peter was silent as he rubbed her wrists gently.

Ada kissed him on the cheek. "You must think I'm taking this Lancelot thing a little too far."

"I was really worried, Ada," he confessed.

She wrapped her arms around him. As they held each other, Peter's eyes traveled to the various photos affixed to Quinn's refrigerator door, most of which were of the woman he now embraced.

OYSTER

"I understand," he said as he extended his hand towards Peter. "Sorry we're meeting under such circumstances. I didn't mean to be...well, I was just expecting Ada to come alone."

"I couldn't get into it on the phone," Ada interjected, "but once you hear what's happened, you'll understand why I think Peter needs to be here."

Jaime cleared his throat, "Does he know?"

Ada nodded. "I showed him what was in the bag. Maybe now you can tell us where you found it."

"My desk," Jaime gave a hopeless laugh. "How it got there, I have no idea!"

"The cigar was just sitting there?"

"Not exactly. I was cleaning off my desk, just pushing around the piles of paper and accumulated crap, and there it was among the mess."

"Didn't you tell me you thought it arrived with travel flyers from Fiesta Cruises Lines," Ada probed.

Jaime hesitated, glancing quickly in Peter's direction. "Right. I'm pretty sure I remember this package arriving, but I was so swamped that I tossed it on the heap. A few pamphlets spilled out. I thought it was entertaining that Santos' company was even marketing to staffers. As if we got paid enough to take vacations." Jaime shrugged, "I probably discarded the envelope when the stuff fell out. I had forgotten about it until yesterday's desk excavation unearthed the brochures and the cigar. It could have come from elsewhere, but they were sort of together. I'd be a pretty big coincidence, especially considering…"

"Considering what?" Ada interrupted.

Frank snapped his finger, as though finally remembering something, but gestured for Jaime to continue.

"Santos' first business in the U.S. was cigar importation – *Cohibas* from the Dominican Republic."

"Really?" she asked.

"He doesn't publicize it. I just know because my boss. Well, they go back a way…"

"Jaime," Peter jumped in, "can you think of any reason for someone to be searching your friend Quinn's apartment?"

"What? Has something happened?"

Ada told him about the break-in and her brief captivity. After finishing, she asked if Jaime knew what Quinn had been working on before he left.

Jaime shook his head. "Not really. I mean Quinn asked for background information on one of the Banking Committee's ongoing investigations. He was interested in the ascendency of a Russian syndicate in international financial transactions. We've been holding hearings for over a year, but it's proving very difficult to distinguish myth from reality. I gave him all the public transcripts and some contacts at Treasury."

"Is that the assignment he's on then," Ada probed, "dirty money in former Eastern Bloc?"

"As near as I can tell. He said something about being stoked to see Prague finally."

"How specific were his questions?" Peter asked.

Jaime stared off, trying to remember: "Not very. He mostly just wanted the minutes from the hearings."

The three fell silent.

"Oh my God," Jaime's fist struck the table, "I can't believe I forgot."

"What?" Peter and Ada both jumped.

"I told you those bills in the cigars were fakes. I suppose I knew that because I'd just been reading about Treasury's new Super Cs. You see, I had to go back to ask the Committee staff for a particular week's hearing notes. I thought I'd given Quinn everything, but he rang to say that one session was missing from the pile. I don't know if I neglected to include it or if the staff messed up, but I had to go back to them. They were kind of pissed. Anyhow, I arranged to meet Quinn to pass them on, but he was late. I passed the time by flipping through the testimony. It was all about the source and circulation of counterfeit $100 bills. Apparently, these fakes, the Super Cs, started showing up just after the new design, which was supposed to be totally counterfeit-proof, was released."

Chapter 10

OPEN MARKETS

"Glaze speaking."
   "You have returned. Was the journey fruitful?"
   "Perhaps."
   "Yes."
   "Yes? Will you agree to meet me?"
   "I want to hear what you found."
   "Buried treasure on the high seas."
   "Ah. And you are being literal are you not?"
   "Indeed."
   "You discovered Monopoly money. Yes?"
   "No. Real. Is that a surprise?"
   "Hmm. Not really. The odds were even."
   "I'm lost..."
   "I will explain, but not now. I must go."
   "Wait! What about our meeting?"
   "Do you know where the stone Prometheus lies?"
   "The statue? The one at the tip of Haines Point?"
   "Tomorrow at dawn. Stand at his right hand. I'll find you."
CLICK
CLICK
   (click)

BIG BEN

Results from a LEXIS-NEXIS search:

Newsday *The United States Treasury Department has begun circulating the first redesigned paper money in 66 years. The new currency features a larger, off-center portrait of Benjamin Franklin, a watermark, special inks, and other hard-to-copy attributes. Treasury, not normally an organization that seeks publicity, spent more than $12 million at home and in other countries preparing people for these new $100 notes, which are designed to thwart sophisticated counterfeiters. Some of the steps that Treasury has taken over the past year to support introduction of redesigned bill introduction include:*

> ➤ *Millions of brochures and posters in over 40 languages, distributed to banks in dozens of countries, from Brazil to Uzbekistan.*

> ➤ *Special training videos to familiarize foreign bank tellers and cash handlers with verification techniques.*

> ➤ *Hotlines to take questions about the bills. The Moscow hotline alone has apparently received between 150 to 200 calls per day.*

Overseas, Treasury officials say they have relied heavily on American embassies and consulates to get the word out. Their main goal is to assure people that their old $100 bills are still valid. Old bills gradually will be replaced with new ones, as they

*wear out and are returned to the U.S. Federal Reserve for
destruction.*

Time Magazine *(Excerpt) The enlarged portrait makes the bill
easier to recognize, while added details make it harder to
replicate. A special micro printing technique is used to make the
words very small and difficult to copy. On the front of the note,
"USA 100" is contained within the number in the lower-left
corner, and "United States of America" is woven into Franklin's
coat. A polymer thread is embedded vertically in the paper. Its
position indicates the note's denomination. The words "USA 100"
on the thread can be seen from both sides of the banknote when it
is held under ultraviolet light. The number in the lower-right
corner on the front of the note looks green when viewed straight
on, but appears black when viewed at an angle...*

Financial Times *(Editorial) United States Administration officials
continue to deny persistent reports that so-called "Super Cs" have
created a counterfeit crisis abroad. The Super Cs are near-perfect
copies of the newly redesigned American 100-dollar bill.*

*High-ranking Federal Reserve officers attempted to
discount the problem in recent testimony before the House Banking
Committee. Nearly two years earlier, however, Secret Service
agents urged officials at the Treasury Department to allocate more
resources to fight counterfeiting, according to a memo obtained
through a Freedom of Information Act request. Currently, the
Secret Service has only five agents working from their Paris
bureau to combat counterfeiting in Europe. From 1992 to 1993,
the counterfeiting caseload in the Paris office nearly doubled.*

*Effective suppression of counterfeiting operations requires
an immediate response and sustained investigation, argued
Professor Ronald Hamilton of the Warton School in sworn
testimony before the House Banking Committee: "When Secret
Service agents are given the resources and top-level support
warranted, they can be remarkably successful. When additional
agents were deployed to Latin America, more than $25 million in
bogus U.S. currency was seized by the local Bogota field office
within weeks." As a publication devoted to strengthening financial
instruments and structures worldwide, the Editors implore the*

Treasury Department to stop playing ostrich. Copy artists have already developed mastery in duplicating the new $100 bills. They must launch a full-scale effort to stop Ben Franklin's enlarged mug from appearing on phony money and weakening the foundation of a strong and trustworthy dollar.

Reuters (North America) *The U.S. House of Representatives Committee on Banking and Financial Services held hearings today on whether a team of U.S officials pressured a top Russian currency expert into retracting statements he made regarding the extent of counterfeit American currency in his country.*

Last month, Anatoly Uskov, former director of foreign exchange for the Russian Central Bank, published an article in The Journal of World Affairs, *stating that the circulation of counterfeit American dollars in Russia is far more serious than American officials have admitted. He mocked the much-heralded introduction of the redesigned $100 bill. The new currency was unveiled in Russia earlier this week, along with a public relations campaign to acclimate the Russian public to the change.*

In his article, Uskov expressed great concern over the state of the Russian banking system, citing estimates that anywhere between 50 to 80 percent of Russian banks are under the control of organized crime. He reported that in the past two years, over $40 billion had been imported into the country, a large part of which, he suspects, is being used for illegal purposes. Uskov also noted that of the $15-20 billion dollars of U.S. currency in Russia, 15-20 percent is counterfeit. If true, this amount would exceed the entire value of ruble notes in current circulation in Russia.

American dollars are by far the most popular hard currency in Russia, representing more than two-thirds of the $390 billion in U.S. currency circulated outside of the United States.

RATES OF EXCHANGE

For the second time that month, Ada marveled at how quickly time seemed to have flown. Welcoming Frank back, sitting again in his den of eccentricities, she experienced a sense of homecoming. Now she was introducing Jaime to Frank. What a turn of events. They all seemed bound together now by fortune's concentric circles.

Frank's escapades on the cruise ship and the cigar-wrapped revelations – both Frank's and Jaime's – had been shared and discussed. Peter had also brought Frank up to speed on the dangerous, but fortunately ham-handed, attempt to hold Ada hostage at Quinn's apartment.

Frank's face reddened with anger. Ada moved to his side and bent down to whisper: "I think Peter rather liked playing the knight on the white steed."

"Should we call the police? I don't want to put any of you in harm's way."

Peter and Jaime began to speak at once, but Ada held up her hand. "Truly, it's alright. I think it was just a strange twist of events, and the man fled. I don't think there'd be much for the cops to do anyhow."

The others seemed to assent.

"Well, I want to reiterate, let's all be cautious." Frank cleared his throat: "Right then. Theories? Conclusions?"

"My captor spoke very rapid Spanish. I'm guessing, based on my brief exposure in Miami, that it was a Cuban accent," Ada began.

"What else," Frank probed.

"He was nervous, tentative, and disorganized."

"Fair to say he wasn't a professional. But did he never let on what he was looking for?"

"No, but we think that, given Jaime's insights, the hunt was connected to Quinn's investigation of Russian syndicates and counterfeiting."

"You said you'd seen him before, Ada?"

"Yes, a couple of weeks ago, when I came off the metro looking for Peter's place. I'd realized that I was heading off in the wrong direction, so I turned around quickly and charged right into the guy. He was bundled up in a coat, gloves, and a hat, which got knocked off. He picked it up and rushed off."

"Can you be sure it was the same person?" Frank asked.

Ada chose her words carefully: "Well, there was a look about him. When he started staring at me in Quinn's flat, it gave me the same creepy feeling that I had on the street in Peter's neighborhood. It was as if the man was looking through me at something else. I don't know if he was drugged, hypnotized, or involved in some devotional task, but there was some inner force propelling him. He seemed to be moving in a trance."

"Isn't that a bit much," Jaime said skeptically, "you got all this from a bump in the street and a few moments of him looking at you?"

"His whole vibe was hard to forget. The eyes were the same." Ada leaned forward, "plus, he recognized me too. That's when he started to panic."

"That's when he had you call me?" Peter prompted.

"Exactly. He knew your name and that I worked with you."

Frank cut in: "You said he wanted 'evidence'?"

Ada shrugged. "That's what he said."

They sat in silence for some time.

"You know," Peter began, "Ada's given me an idea about our fretful zealot." Turning towards Frank, he asked: "wasn't there a commando group that used to patrol around the Everglades firing paint slugs at Fidel and Raul Castro effigies?"

"Weekend warriors?" Ada joked.

"No," Jaime cut in soberly. He hesitated. "It's not a game to them. It's deadly serious. I know about that group. They are supposedly preparing an invasion of the island and the restoration of a pre-Revolutionary order."

It was Frank who continued. "That's right. Their swamp training camp may sound amateurish, but these people mean business. The ultimate goal is to be successful where the Bay of Pigs veterans (their fathers, in many cases) failed. They blame the Kennedy brothers, weak-kneed liberals, and traitorous Communist sympathizers from their own country, for the loss in '61. They've vowed to defeat any effort that directly or indirectly legitimizes the current regime."

Jaime picked up the thread: "The group has sent bombs to the offices of organizations that support normalizing relations with Cuba. Anyone who is helping to prop up Castro, in their eyes, is the enemy."

"Could this guy be one of them?" Ada asked.

"Fits the profile," Peter said. "It doesn't explain why he was tailing you the first time though."

"And it doesn't fully explain why he was in Quinn's flat."

Frank nodded. "I should add one more detail about these people. They may sound silly, but they are essentially a paramilitary group. They've taken their name from the mythology of the exile community and its hero – the one who allegedly shook off Castro's chains and flew to freedom. They call themselves: *Los Murcielagos, The Batmen*."

Ada, Frank, and Peter looked at one another. Jaime stared at his hands.

A gong echoed throughout the room.

INSIDE TRADE

Frank wasn't long at the door. The visitor had been quick, but Frank took a few minutes afterwards in his study. In their host's absence, Peter had given Jaime a tour of the study, noting some of the finer objects, explaining which people had fashioned them and why. Ada walked along behind, thinking about Peter's parents. They had wandered far and wide, worked hard, and led independent, unconventional lives, though they had shared none of that with their son. Peter had been excluded from their adventures, whereas Frank brought him in, teaching him rhyming slang, drawing maps, reenacting dances, parroting dialects – just as Peter was doing now with Jaime.

Peter could easily have become an awkward loner, indifferent autocrat, or inflexible egoist. And yet, he was generous, understanding, and kind. Peter had made Ada feel a part of his life, without assigning her a station, restricting her movements, or assessing a toll. It occurred to her that she'd have cause to be terrified or at least alarmed about recent events in her life, but excitement and a sense of purpose were the only sensations she felt, and the stirrings of something beyond.

"Where were we then?" Frank coughed. Peter and Jaime broke from their discussion of the morality of pharmaceutical companies hiring Shaman to help prospect for medicinal plants. Ada also returned from her private thoughts.

"What's up?" Peter smiled.

"Nothing important. I'll have to run off in a bit, but let's finish up here. Shall we have a look at those *Cohibas* now, Mr. Acosta?"

Jaime reached into his jacket pocket and withdrew the bag containing the split tobacco leaf and the crisp counterfeit greenbacks, which Ada had returned to him.

"They are fake, but plenty good enough to fool most people. I'm pretty sure these are what Treasury is calling "Super Cs," the best forgeries in current circulation." He placed the bag in Frank's hand.

"But the notes that Frank found on the boat were real, weren't they?" Jaime asked.

Frank leaned back, stretching his legs across a silken sea of Turkish threadwork. "Yes, that's the most baffling aspect of this odd coincidence. Or confluence. It's not so much that we both found money in cigars, but that some are decoys and some the real McCoy."

"More like the real McClellan," Peter quipped with a sly smile.

"Ah," Frank chuckled proudly. "Yes, we could use a touch of that Union soldier's luck." Turning to the others, he continued: "McClellan found General Lee's Antietam battle plans on a piece of paper wrapped around three cigars."

"Actual battlefield intelligence would come in handy right now," Jaime enjoined.

"He's right. We've amassed the clues, but it seems like we're stuck on the surface of their meaning. We need to get underneath." Hesitating, Ada continued, "I've been thinking, maybe we should consider reaching out to Quinn. He might help fit some pieces of the puzzle."

Jaime answered first. "One problem will be getting in touch with him. When I dropped him at the airport, he gave the impression he'd be on the move. He was literally carrying a single backpack. Plus, as you know Ada, he'll be protective of his story," he said carefully.

"I know," she sighed. "I just thought we could pitch it like a trade. Like Frank did with Brooke Glaze. They joined forces. Her journalistic instincts led her to see the benefit of an exchange. Maybe Quinn would react the same way. Enlightened self-interest…"

Jaime pondered this. Peter too appeared to be considering these points. Frank's face bore the look of one who has just recalled an important task, his body projecting motion before he'd even risen.

"I don't see how it could hurt to try, Ada. The worst your friend could say is 'no.' Give it a go." With that, Frank stood and moved towards the door. "Terribly rude. I apologize, but I simply must run out and take care of something. Please, continue" Frank motioned for them to remain.

"It's worth a try." Jaime concluded, after Frank had left.

Ada nodded. "I might have better luck finding Quinn, if I go through his father, rather than his editor."

"Senator Keegan has always been a sucker for your charms." Jaime teased.

Had Frank lingered in the room long enough to hear this exchange, he might well have sought to derail Ada's plan. Frank, however, was already headed up Wisconsin Avenue with a small key in his coat pocket.

BEAST IN THE JUNGLE

Frank waited for the sun to rise over the granite, limestone, and marble of the Washington Mall. From Haines Point, where he stood, he could just mark the great monuments silhouetted behind the thinning fog. Mist blew across the Potomac River towards Virginia. Frank knelt in a bed of sodden pine needles, hidden by the chaste draping of a mulberry bush.

A single gull passed overhead, as the arc of headlights cut the morning haze. The hum of an engine moved slowly closer. The vehicle came to rest roughly 25 feet from Frank's secluded waiting place. A door shut and footfall on the gravel marked a lone figure's approach. Frank watched the newcomer circle the massive five-piece form, which graced the Point. The statue featured Prometheus' proud head, bent knee, twisted leg, reaching forearm, and supplicant hand. The woman passed her own hand across the pleading palm. Pausing, she surveyed the area. Frank could see her inhale and he marked the release of her breath as it grew visible in the cold air. He could tell she was shivering. A twinge of guilt over hiding plucked at his sense of honor. She would understand, he hoped. Forgiveness was another matter.

They lingered separately, each waiting for the dawn to break, hoping that the appointment one of them made would materialize.

Brightness took the morning sky in layers. The ground seemed to shift with the warming of the sun. Frank and the woman who's rendezvous he was crashing also stirred, both becoming more alert. They were still alone in this spot, though sounds of accelerated activity in the surrounding city carried more swiftly. Shortly, the crunch of tires on asphalt bit the last slice of solitude. A silver Jaguar swung into view, gaining on them at a steady purr. The 12-cylinder motor took one stately turn around the statue, before pulling off to a patch of earth equidistant between Brooke (for it was indeed her) by the statue and Frank in his hiding place.

Nearly a minute passed before the legs of the driver met the ground. Even at a distance, Frank could admire the cut of the sharply tailored suit. A long, slim skirt of some dark fabric and fitted jacket accentuated the woman's graceful gait. She moved with purpose but not speed. If the scene were being filmed, the director would have held the camera on that walk an extra moment to make the point. As it was, Frank sensed he'd seen this sequence before, if not on screen, then in a dream. Distracted, he didn't notice the arrival of a third vehicle, until it swerved into his line of vision. With startling swiftness, a large man emerged from the passenger seat, grabbed the new arrival from behind, and forced her to walk towards his car.

Frank had been crouching so long in the bushes that he felt paralyzed. He tried to make out the face of the driver. He looked to Brooke, who appeared frozen with shock. Her helplessness galvanized him. Frank stood, preparing to leap from his lair, but in rising, his coat had become snagged and he slipped on the dewy ground. Hearing this commotion, the captor tried to pick the woman up, but she used this opportunity to resist. Pulling away, she ran a few steps. He caught up to her, twisting her wrist as he did so. The woman stumbled, emitting a cry of pain. The fall had claimed her cloche hat and what remained of her strength. The man lifted her into the backseat and swung the door shut. The car sped off, leaving her vehicle, a wall of dust, and the fine bell-shaped hat, which had hidden the woman's face until the final moment.

Frank fell with a thud upon the path. The stubborn vine that had derailed his act of heroism still clung to him. Its thorny protest recorded red scratches across his face and hands. Brooke, unaware of his presence during the abduction, called out. Anger, her initial reaction, changed quickly to alarm as she noticed the bloody scrapes. She wanted to tend to him, but something about Frank's bearing made her reluctant to intrude. He began to writhe in pain, displaying an agony far deeper than any flesh wound could cause. Brook watched, as he clutched the dirt moaning, his face a mask of sorrow.

Brooke turned away. The statue of the titan Prometheus – punished for stealing Zeus's fire and giving it to humans – lay before her. The mythical champion of mankind, who had defined the gods, was chained to a rock. An eagle would return each day to tear out the liver that grew back again every night. The sculptor had captured well both the despair and the valor of the Promethean struggle to be free.

She could still hear Frank sobbing. Brooke closed her eyes. She squeezed them shut, trying to block out the image of him reaching out for an answer to a question she didn't yet understand.

Chapter 11

TALON

"Do you think you can make a fool of me?"

"You flatter me too much, dear cousin. You do not need my help in that regard."

"Everything. I gave you everything. All any woman could want. I brought you to this country, bought you a beautiful home, jewels, and servants. But stare is all you do. You never cared about the things I shower upon you. Ungrateful witch. Never once have you deigned to show me thanks or affection. I am your husband, blood of your ancestors, but you have never loved me, never tried to hide your hatred. Now, I find you betraying me and your people to the enemy...."

"I?" she spoke with the bitter force and speed of a dam breaking. "You dare to talk to me of love and betrayal? You, who forced me to forsake my heart, tore it from my breast to claim it as your own? You, whose whole life is a façade, a perverse game, a mockery of human courage and virtue? Yes, it is true that I have worked to expose you and the hideous evil beneath your lies. I want to speak the secrets that have imprisoned me. How I have longed to tell the world that I went to you, my cousin, desperate for your help, but uncovered a wicket ruse. Fidel had rejected you for the self-serving hypocrite that you are. The revolution had no use for you, so you used it. Used it to reinvent yourself in the new world. Revenge, control over others, that is all you love. Don't speak to me of loyalty and gratitude. The words are poisoned by your tongue. I begged you to help me join the man I loved in

200

America, and you tricked me. You made me send that hateful letter. You told me my parents had been killed. You brought me here for your own use. How could I have believed you? I must have been mad. I am surely crazy now."

He laughed cruelly. "And so, puta, you have discovered that your Yanqui is alive. You have decided to destroy yourself and me in a pitiful act of redemption. You are a fool."

"I did read of him," her voice catching, "in the newspaper. But this is not about him. It is about you. I can no longer harden my eyes to your crimes. Your wickedness is not just the trickery of an attention-seeking child. You and your minions are thieves. And worse. You steal from your own people."

"That is enough! My minions, as you say, are warriors in a noble battle. My Batmen fight traitors like you."

"Let them kill me. I died years ago by my own hand, the day I wrote that letter."

"Spare me your tears. All this time, you have clung to an illusion. The Yanqui would have tired of his exotic girl soon enough," he seethed. "You think I was never good enough for you. Now you will be good for no one."

She stood to meet her fate. A lost prophet on a burning shore.

ROUND UP

Peter nudged the door wider with his bare foot, trying not to spill anything. He moved gingerly to where Ada lay. Still holding the tray, he stood admiring her ability to rest so peacefully. Not a trace of concern marred her brow. Slowly, she opened her eyes to find his face above her.

"Come back to bed."

Peter set breakfast aside and did as he was told.

The telephone rudely interrupted.

"Not again?!" Ada exclaimed, "What was that Yogi Berra line?

"Ain't over 'til…"

"That's much better than the one I was thinking of!" she cooed, "extra innings beat *déjà vu* hands down."

"Hold that thought," he pulled her hand towards his mouth to kiss it, as he spoke into the receiver.

"Hey, Ben…" Peter's face grew more serious, "I don't know. Brooke Glaze and she's...what? And Frank?" Listening, Peter murmured assent periodically then repeated his instructions: "I understand. I'm to tell him you know all about it and that he's to be there if he wants answers." He paused, "Right, I'll take care of it."

Peter put the phone down. "We need to get dressed. Ben's called a pow wow for 9am. His office. You hop in the shower. I have to make a quick call."

Ada slipped out of the sheets. "What was all that about Frank and Brooke?"

"Not sure. Ben seems to think Frank may be in some kind of troubled state. Ben wants me to communicate to Frank that he knows the way out."

"Frank was fine the day before yesterday."

Peter smiled at her naked form, "Get going before I'm further distracted by your charms."

"I'll be speedy," she called out, bounding out of bed and padding into the bathroom.

He watched her go, then picked up the phone.

THE BULL AND THE BEAR

It being a Saturday, the corridors of Congress were deserted. The silence of the halls seemed to intensify as the couple's hurried footsteps struck the floor. Ada listened self-consciously. The door to Ben O. Davey's outer office was closed. Peter's knock was answered by the distinguished gentleman himself. He greeted them with a relieved expression, ushering them quickly through the suite to his inner office. Ada entered first.

A man sat, at ease, in the large leather armchair beside Ben's desk. He rose upon seeing her, dominating the space with his physical presence. Everything about him was designed to impress and intimidate. This wasn't the first time she'd taken that in.

Ada realized she was blocking the door and took a step forward.

"Hello, Ada," the tall man began to bend his frame, his jaw softening to reveal a bright white line of teeth. She gave him a hesitant hug.

She squinted slightly, searching for the proper words, "What a surprise." Ada moved further into the room, giving herself time to think and the others space to enter. "How is Quinn," she probed, "is everything okay?"

"Quinn is fine, dear. I'll explain my presence in a moment," he caught Ben's eye.

"Let's wait for the others to arrive before we begin."

The others, Ada wondered. With an awkwardly formal gesture, she motioned, "Senator Keegan, may I introduce you to Peter Vane."

"Pleased to meet you, Mr. Vane." The men shook hands. Whether to put the younger at ease or for some more intricate purpose, Senator Keegan leaned forward in a confiding manner. "I can't say that I've always agreed with COG's agenda, but I have been favorably impressed by your impact. Soft money contributions weren't such a problem in my day. I've found your reports to be balanced and thoughtful."

Peter shifted his weigh. It was the flattery that unsettled him, Ada observed, not the proximity of a taller man or the discomfort of meeting the father of her former lover.

"Glad that we made an impression," Peter responded with only a trace of irony.

Ben interrupted. "Is Frank on the way?"

"I believe so," Peter's eyes found Ada. He moved to sit at her side before continuing, "I gave him your message."

Ben knotted his brow, motioning for further comment. He looked tired and constrained. They were the ones who should be asking the questions, Ada thought to herself.

Peter shrugged and added. "I gave him the message, and he hurried me off the phone. I assume he'll show up, though he sounded ..." He cleared his throat with a short cough, and shot a look at Senator Keegan, in whose presence he had no desire to break confidences.

"I apologize," came a familiar voice. "I let myself in," Frank explained as he crossed the carpet into the Congressman's office.

Frank greeted them each in turn, coming to the Senator last without extending his hand: "Lewis, it's been some time."

"Yes, yes it has," the other agreed.

Peter broke the silence that followed. "Ben, may I ask why we're all assembled here," he inquired.

Frank remained standing. He placed a hand on his godson's shoulder.

"Perhaps the Senator can fill us in on what's going on." Color began to rise in Frank's face; his voice seemed gripped by a strange edge. "I assume it's his lot that have been listening in on my calls. Unmarked vans tend to stand out in my neighborhood."

Ben spoke defensively. "Frank, I knew nothing about all this until an hour ago." He tilted his head towards Quinn's father, "Senator, this is your show. You have some explaining to do."

Senator Keegan gave the group a wry smile. "As soon as the others arrive, I shall begin."

"What others?" Frank asked.

"Brooke Glaze and May Scully."

The two women entered the room, as if on cue.

It was clear they had arrived together. "Good Morning," May spoke first.

"Sorry to keep you waiting," Brooke added in a clipped voice.

Ben indicated for them to be seated.

BATTING A THOUSAND

The Senator began to pace with his hands clasped loosely behind his back. "There are many ways that an individual serves his or her country," he began pedantically. "In my case, as a legislator and, more recently, as a private citizen involved in various philanthropic endeavors…" A restless rustle moved through the room, "There are other outlets, other means, shall we say, at the disposal of one who still possesses certain skills or knowledge. These are tools, which one may lend when national security requires. This," he punctuated the lecture with a dramatic sigh, "is why you have been called here."

"Summoned," Frank muttered.

"As you will," the Senator acknowledged respectfully. "Your 'summons' concerns a call from your country. You may think of it as a special service you are being asked to render. First and foremost, your absolute silence is essential. Lives depend upon this." The Senator retook his seat and leaned back, "may I be assured of your cooperation?"

"Excuse me?" Frank broke in, "this is damned presumptuous!"

The Senator spoke calmly: "Frank, I have always respected, and defended, I'll remind you, your independence of mind and action." He gave a moment for this reference and its implication to sink in before continuing: "Even so, the circumstances here are highly unusual. They concern interests far greater than individual egos, principled or otherwise. I must insist."

Frank slapped the arm of the chair. "Look, it's perfectly clear who you're working for. Before I pledge my allegiance to your rogue outfit, I want to know why." He rose from his seat. "You needn't remind me that there is a history between us. I have leverage too, Lewis."

Maintaining his tone of icy calm, Senator Keegan sought to steer the conversation back. "Some of the others may not yet have grasped the meaning of our discussion. Shall we allow them to catch up?"

"Yes," Frank retorted, "Tell them the truth *before* you gag them. I'm quite certain Ms. Glaze isn't about to take an oath of silence without a hint as to why. She's a reporter, for Christ sake."

Brooke made no motion, but her unmoving gaze punctuated Frank's point.

Senator Keegan remained silent, waiting.

"This is bullshit," Frank exploded with an edge of hysteria, "Tell me what you've done with her?" The others exchanged looks of alarm.

"You misunderstand," the Senator shot back, "the kidnapping is not our affair."

Frank, jagged with strain: "That is a lie."

Senator Keegan threw up his hands and cast an exasperated face at Ben, who turned away. Ada and Peter, looking utterly confused, glanced around for answers. Brooke began to stand, but May's tug guided her to remain. It was Quinn's father who broke the tension.

"Frank," he spoke with finality. "You don't have another choice but to trust me, so let's cut to the chase."

"That's what I've been asking for," Frank replied quietly. "Tell me where she is."

Ben had moved over to put his hand on his friend's shoulder. "Please, Frank. You have every right to be upset and angry, but it's time to listen." He lowered his voice, "You need them, like it or not. It's the only way to help her now."

Frank's mouth went dry. He set his jaw and fixed his eyes on the wall opposite. "Proceed."

After a beat, the Senator resumed. "Through actions that were not only reckless, but exceedingly dangerous, you have uncovered certain information about the activities of one Miguel Santos, cruise ship company founder and prominent leader in the Cuban-American exile community. This individual's involvement in illegal operations – primarily, counterfeiting and money laundering – began shortly after Mr. Santos' arrival on our shores. This much, I believe, in part, you have discovered. The United States clandestine service, as you may or may not know, has had him under surveillance since day-one."

"Under surveillance for more than three decades? Surely, you must have gathered enough evidence to convict him, if you'd been remotely interested in doing so?" Brooke cut in sarcastically.

"Of course, Ms. Glaze," the Senator responded. "However, there were overriding interests that made public revelation undesirable."

"You mean the likely fact that Mr. Santos' criminal ties were first formed in league with the U.S. Central Intelligence Agency?" goaded Peter.

"Elementary, but rather beside the point. We are not here to debate history or morality. There is not enough time." Senator Keegan drew a deep breath, "The facts can't be changed. Operation Mongoose was a reality. The President and his wise men wanted Castro gone. The Agency failed on its own. It turned to the mob and the exile community for help. This rag tag band of mercenaries and evangelists tried assassinations, invasions, and all manner of botched attempts. For their trouble, they sent America down a path of perpetual antagonism towards Cuba. Their mistakes pushed Castro further into the arms of our Great Red Nemesis, prompting a missile crisis with the Soviets, etc., etc. This just further bred delusions of grandeur among this cohort and their gangland associates. So, the CIA found itself with a compounded problem. A stronger Castro, an angrier Khrushchev, a loose-cannon group of exiles, mobsters holding national secrets, and at the center of the pile, a self-declared hero of Napoleonic ego and ambition, Miguel Santos."

The weight of these failures seemed to have wearied the Senator's handsome features. He sucked air through his teeth slowly, creating a discordant whistle, before plunging back in. "We could argue a lifetime…many have, regarding the wisdom or hubris of these actions. That's not the issue now. We have a much more serious and immediate concern on our hands." With a nod to Ben and Frank, he continued: "Let me get to the point. The Agency's past relationship with Santos, as well as America's overall policy towards a Castro-led Cuba, made it necessary to turn a blind eye to Santo's activities. The benefits of exposing him were weighed against the cost of public scandal. As you might expect, the Agency chose to remain silent."

"Lewis?" Ben prodded.

"Yes. The Agency has been complicit, as well as silent." The Senator looked at each of them directly. "It is at this juncture that I must really insist upon your secrecy."

Slowly, all heads nodded acceptance.

"Intelligence operatives have assisted in the suppression of information. They have hidden from other sectors of the government knowledge of air and sea traffic between the mainland and the island of Cuba. They have shielded a large web of activity in the Caribbean directly tied to Santos' illegal operations."

"The pilot defections?" Ben asked.

Pressing further, Peter added: "And the amendments regarding broadcasts…were those designed to keep comings and goings under wraps?"

"There is only one aerostat – one working radar balloon – in South Florida. Giving priority to the propaganda broadcasts would preempt its used by the Defense Department, Customs, and Treasury…"

"What has been coming and going?" Brooke cut in.

"Santos was counterfeiting U.S. dollars from the beginning. His syndicate sponsors set him up with a couple of cigar factories, which functioned as fronts for printing operations. He'd press the greenbacks, roll them into tobacco leaves as cover, and ship them to the Dominican Republic for distribution, primarily to the Soviet Union and Eastern Bloc countries, where they'd circulate quite freely on the closed black market." The Senator paused to shake his head. "Having demonstrated his loyalty and hungry for more action, Santos branched out from there, pulling in mob associates to back a more sophisticated money laundering operation, using the cruise ships' physical mobility and liquid casino business to move money from illegal outlets to seemingly legitimate holdings."

"Still counterfeiting too?" Ada asked.

"It ran like a back-and-forth. Phony flowed out, dirty flowed in. Santos still sent crates of counterfeit bills to the D.R., but by the

1980s, he was also bringing in criminal earnings in real currency, similarly wrapped. He'd just unload the hidden loot when docked back in Miami, funnel it through as house winnings from the ship's betting tables, or wash it through banks, currency exchange outlets, and brokerage houses. He'd take his cut in the form of cashier's checks or offshore wire transfers, or he'd use deposits as collateral for legitimate investments. He's even used the Cuban American Liberation Bond as a vehicle, making $100,000 donations in the name of hundreds of individuals, who couldn't possibly have contributed such amounts on their own."

"Why the pangs of remorse?" Brooke asked.

"Pardon?"

Holding the Senator's gaze, Brooke spelled it out: "What's changed the Agency's tune?

"There is a very real concern that Santos is straying beyond the bounds of the acceptable..."

"Acceptable being a relative term."

"Yes, Ms. Glaze. Santos is moving off of the reservation to a field less containable than mere financial improprieties. The fall of the Soviet Union brought many underground forces to the surface. The thaw has brought old KGB and Soviet secret police into alliance with Italian mafia, Columbian cartels, etc. Russian crime organizations are also now involved in human trafficking, nuclear arms sales, internet insecurity, intellectual property theft...energy, oil, wherever there is money to be made and power to be amassed. No longer just a puppet counter-revolutionary tinkering with Treasury notes, Santos has become a link in a much larger chain encircling the globe. Now, this may all be reversable. The Agency is counting on the fact that Santos is so cocky that he may be playable. We want to use him as the lure to catch bigger fish."

"You're asking us to back off so you can use him to set a trap?" Ada challenged.

"This goes far beyond campaign finance violations, counterfeiting, and money laundering. We're talking about a movement towards global control of the world's civil, monetary, and nuclear security. There is no choice in this matter. There can be no press, no reports, no references, no discussion. Nothing. Absolute silence is the only way we will ensnare Santos. We must lull him into a false sense of security."

An ominous "or else" hung above the group. Fill in your own blank, it said.

Without lifting his head, Frank spoke: "What about her?"

Ben caught Peter's eye before blinking nervously. Beating back the urge to stand up again, he leaned forward.

Senator Keegan also shifted uncomfortably. "We'll get her back. We'll do it our own way though, Frank."

"Who is she?" Ada whispered, almost to herself.

Frank shook his head, "She…."

No one said a word for many moments. Senator Keegan then cut in briskly: "Of course, these are private matters. From what we understand, Carolina Olazabal entered the United States shortly before the so-called miraculous arrival of Miguel Santos to Key West. His much-heralded escape from prison was, we know without a shadow of a doubt from surveillance reports, complete hogwash. Upon arrival on U.S. shores, Santos presented INS officials with a marriage certificate dated days prior from Havana. His wife was located, and the couple brought together at a Customs facility in Miami. The woman had been held for psychological evaluation by the intake officer, who thought she might," the Senator hesitated, "harm herself." The officer had taken a statement from the woman alleging that she had been kidnapped by the devil and forced to eat her own heart. The officer took this as a sign of delirium. It was at this point that they put her case on hold and called in the shrinks. Doctors never had a chance to examine her, however, as Santos showed up to claim her. So, they released her to him and put her ravings down to the trauma common among newly-arrived refugees."

"This is Santos' wife we're talking about?" May asked.

"His wife and distant cousin," Senator Keegan confirmed, adding: "On the few occasions in which she had appeared with him publicly, her distaste for him was palpable. There are no children. We are given to understand that she is more prisoner than spouse."

Silence grew around them as this story sunk in. No one wanted to break the hush that seemed to belong most profoundly to Frank. They waited. When he finally lifted his face, he appeared oddly peaceful, saying almost to himself: "She was trying to destroy him."

Senator Keegan hesitated. "Yes, that's our impression. Her efforts to put Ms. Glaze on the scent and her attempt to meet Ms. Glaze at Haynes Point – these all indicate an intention to reveal what she knew of her husband's criminal affairs. How much she actually knows is unclear, but she wanted to bring him down regardless."

"You can secure her release, you said?" Brooke cut in.

"Yes, but I can say nothing further," he looked at Frank and nodded meaningfully.

"She will no longer be a source, Ms. Glaze. There is no longer a scoop to be had," added the Senator.

"I'm not asking out of concern for my story," Brooke objected.

"My role here is done," Senator Keegan stood abruptly. Before exiting the room, he paused and placed a hand on Ada's shoulder.

UNBOUND

The scene of her sad exile: rugged once
And desolate and frozen, like this ravine:
But now invested with fair flowers and herbs

For forty years, Frank's nocturnal wanderings traversed the same patch of ground. Regardless of when in the dream sequence he would awaken, Frank was always left with the same dull ache in his bones. Asleep, he would search flickering shadows and chase the sound of her voice, but he could never find her before the spell was broken.

Now, he sat terrified. Dreams are not for daylight hours.

Frank had been instructed to wait by the statue of Prometheus. The sculptor had titled his masterpiece of public art *Awakening*.

He felt the stony face looming behind him. Prometheus imagined the apex of human perfection, only to be forced to live with a constant reminder of his folly. In the classical myth, he took the risk and bore the loss. In the 19th century, one of the great Romantic poets Percy Bysshe Shelly revised the tale. Shelly portrayed Prometheus not as a titan but as a man, once whole, who fell into division and struggled for redemption. Shelly replaced the quest for fire with the search for love. His Prometheus represented the very human desire to feel complete. In Shelly's vision, romantic communion was what would release human suffering, fulfill what lay incomplete, and reunite what had been divided.

Chapter 12

SPRING 1996

She stood erect, perfectly still, as the car that had delivered her pulled slowly away.

"Caro?"

A human voice, the first it seemed she'd heard in decades, split the chilly calm. She tried but couldn't stop herself from shaking. The morning sun overwhelmed her sense of sight. The world began to spin. She fainted on the rocky road. She did not feel the hands that lifted her and pressed her close. All was black. But from that senseless pitch, a sound pulled her back.

"Caro, Caro, Caro."

A chant to raise the dead. Again.

"Caro, Caro, Caro."

Her skin awakened to the pressure of his touch. She blinked away tears. His eyes held her. Blue like the Caribbean. Bright like the beginnings of all things.

AMBOS MUNDOS

"You're looking at me," she said.

"Can't help myself."

"A girl likes to pout in peace."

"Sorry," drawing her onto his knee, "you are irresistible in any mood."

She began stroking his hair.

"Come on," he nudged, "talk to me."

"I feel silly."

He loosened his grip.

"No, no," she pulled his arms back around her. "I mean that I know I'm being childish for being disappointed." Ada rested her chin on his shoulder. "We got cheated, right?"

"No prize in the Crackerjack box?" he sighed, "yep, that's one way to see it."

"Is there another way? It feels futile to have risked so much, only to be forced into silence. Think about it: Jaime has quit his dream job; Brooke lost a career-making exposé. Quinn did too, I suppose. And, my God, imagine what worse could have happened to Carolina. I can't even think about the pain Frank suffered all those years."

Searching her grey eyes, he spoke the thoughts he'd been turning over in his mind: "Ada, should Jaime have stayed with that creep Peralta? Brooke lost a story, but she met May and they seem pretty happy together. Your buddy Quinn is young; he has years of Pulitzer prize chasing ahead of him and at least he's a continent away from his father. As to Frank and Carolina," he signed, "they have found each other after all this time. Pain must recede with such a gift."

Ada began to tear up. "I know."

He squeezed her hand, "I'm disappointed that we can't bust Santos too," he stopped abruptly. "Actually, I take that back. To hell with it."

Ada stared at him, "What?"

"For years, I've watched the only person who has ever been a parent to me burdened with inner agony. I grew up never wanting to care so much about another person that losing her would mean losing myself. I think now that I was missing the point."

Ada put her hand to his cheek.

"You're divine," said he.

She looked into his eyes and saw all the stories that surround a human life rising and falling like waves around the proverbial desert island. She wasn't sure who was on the sand or in the sea, but she could feel her breath move in rhythm with his. It felt so natural and complete that little else seemed to matter.

"And you are mine," said she.

Fin

Tamsin Spencer Smith, South Florida, circa 1976

Tamsin Spencer Smith is a San Francisco-based poet, painter, and essayist. She's published three collections of poetry: *Word Cave* (Risk Press, 2018); *Between First and Second Sleep* (FMSBW, 2018); and *Displacement Geology* (FMSBW, 2020). Her paintings have been exhibited at various San Francisco venues, including: Adobe Books Backroom Gallery, Modern Eden, The Luggage Store Gallery, Guerrero Gallery, Incline Gallery, and The Midway. Smith also writes art reviews and catalogue essays, the most recent of which, "A Summer Drawing Circle: The Story of Joan Brown's Mary Julia Series" was published by the George Adams Gallery in 2020.

Born in England, Smith grew up in the Coconut Grove neighborhood of Miami. Her mother is a cell biologist and her father was a lepidopterist, who frequently visited friends and scientific colleagues on the island of Cuba. In 1994, he published an illustrated guide and history of the more than 600 species and sub-species of butterflies found in the Caribbean and southern Florida. Smith attended Kenyon College, where she graduated summa cum laude with highest honors in English for her thesis on Vladimir Nabokov.

THE DIVERS COLLECTION

Number 1
Hôtel des Étrangers, poems by **Joachim Sartorius** translated from German to English by **Scott J. Thompson**

Number 2
Making Art, a memoir by **Mary Julia Klimenko**

Number 3
XISLE, a novel by **Tamsin Spencer Smith**

Made in the USA
Middletown, DE
20 November 2022

15561228R00137